A Wint...

Neil was leading Sam ... freezing courtyard whe... ...nought struck him. Where was J... ...here was no sign of the vulnerable little pup.

"Jake! Jake!" he called anxiously. But no little puppy scurried up to answer him. Everything was quiet . . .

The Snow Dog

Neil stood watching as Max walked out on to the ice. Max kept calling the dogs and eventually they both ran towards him. Then Max seemed to stagger and he yelled something Neil couldn't catch. Jake started to bark. As Neil stared, he saw a dark line open in the ice and Max went plunging down into the waters of the lake . . .

Holly's Wish

Suddenly Neil saw a dark shape in the snow ahead of him, directly in his path. He squinted through the snowflakes, trying to work out what it was. Then he realized, and his heart lurched. It was a Labrador puppy and, from what he could see, it was not very old . . .

Titles in the Puppy Patrol® series

All Jenny Dale's PUPPY PATROL® books
can be ordered at your local bookshop or
available by post from Book Service by Post
(tel: 01624 675737).

A Puppy Patrol®
Three-in-One Special
Christmas Cracker!

Jenny Dale

Illustrated by
Mick Reid

A Working Partners Book
MACMILLAN CHILDREN'S BOOKS

*Special thanks to Cherith Baldry
and Liss Norton*

A Winter's Tale first published 1998 by Macmillan Children's Books
The Snow Dog first published 1999 by Macmillan Children's Books
Holly's Wish first published 2000 by Macmillan Children's Books

This edition published 2001 by Macmillan Children's Books
a division of Pan Macmillan Limited
20 New Wharf Road, London N1 9RR
Basingstoke and Oxford
www.panmacmillan.com

Associated companies throughout the world

Created by Working Partners Limited
London W6 0QT

ISBN 0 330 39730 3

1 3 5 7 9 8 6 4 2

A CIP catalogue record for this book is available from
the British Library.

Typeset by SX Composing DTP, Rayleigh, Essex
Printed by Mackays of Chatham plc, Kent

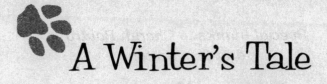

A Winter's Tale

Chapter One

"*Dick Whittington and his Dog?* What sort of pantomime is that?" Neil Parker pointed to a brightly coloured poster on the noticeboard and laughed. "What happened to the cat?"

"Who needs a cat?" his sister Emily said. "Denny's brilliant. He's our star pooch."

Neil and his mother, Carole Parker, along with Neil's five-year-old sister Sarah, had arrived at the church hall in Compton to collect Emily from her pantomime rehearsal. Every year the Compton Amateur Dramatic Society put on a special Christmas show for the local children, and this time Emily had a small part.

Neil had first met Denny, the golden retriever

in the pantomime, when a truck had hit the dog on the road just outside King Street Kennels. Gina Ward, who was in the year below Neil at Meadowbank School, had been walking Denny when the accident had happened. Neil had helped her to look after him while they waited for the vet. He didn't find out how clever Denny was until much later.

"Fudge is brilliant, too," said Sarah. "Why can't he be in the play?"

"*Dick Whittington and his Hamster?*" said Neil. "In your dreams, Squirt."

"Hamsters are too small," added Carole, as Sarah screwed up her face in a sulk. "No one in the audience would be able to see him."

Neil shifted his feet and looked around. The weather was icy cold outside, with snow expected, and the Church Hall felt distinctly chilly inside, even though he was wearing two sweaters, a padded jacket *and* a cap with ear-flaps pulled down over his spiky brown hair. He slapped his hands together in their woollen gloves.

Looking around, Neil could hardly believe that the pantomime would be ready in time for New Year's Eve, just ten days away – or that the cast had already been rehearsing for weeks.

The stage was bare except for a couple of chairs and a table, and the people standing in the middle of it were busy talking amongst themselves, not even trying to rehearse.

At the other end of the hall, Chris and Hasheem, two of Neil's friends from school, were sloshing paint onto a big canvas. In fact, Neil thought, Meadowbank School was well represented; his teacher, Paul Hamley, was there too, perched dangerously at the top of a ladder, fixing one of the stage lights.

"Are you going to be long?" Neil asked Emily. "I want to get back to King Street."

"I don't know."

Neil shifted again and looked impatiently at the hall clock. It was just coming up to half past five. "I've got to be home by six," he said. "Jane Hammond is bringing Jake."

Before Emily could reply, somebody called her, and she dashed off towards the stage. Neil turned back to where Carole was sitting on one of the hall chairs against the wall.

"Mum, I've got to be home by six," he repeated.

Carole was staring in front of her, not taking any notice of Neil. "I've posted the last of the Christmas cards . . ." She ticked the item off on

3

her fingers. "I've collected the turkey. I've bought the veg, the chocolates and – gift wrap! I've forgotten the gift wrap!"

"Oh, Mum . . ."

Carole Parker gathered up her handbag. "Neil, I'm just going to nip down to the High Street before the shops close. Keep an eye on Sarah for me. I won't be long."

"Mum—" Neil protested, but Carole's tall figure was already disappearing out of the hall.

Neil shrugged, and looked round for his little sister. She was waving a brush around, trying to help with the painting but getting more blue paint over herself than on the scenery.

"Mum'll kill me!" Neil groaned as he looked at Sarah's paint-spattered jeans.

He walked down the hall to where the scene painters were at work. Hasheem straightened up, making faces and rubbing his back vigorously.

"Here comes the Puppy Patrol!" he said. "Why aren't you in the pantomime, Neil? There's a dog in it, you know. I didn't think anything could keep you away from dogs."

"You've got to be able to sing," Neil replied. Then he grinned. He was a bit disappointed not

4

to be in the pantomime, but he wasn't going to make a fuss about it.

"And your voice sounds like all the dogs in King Street howling at once." Hasheem chuckled. "That explains a lot."

Neil's parents, Carole and Bob, ran a boarding kennels with a small rescue centre, in the country town of Compton. The thought of all the residents of King Street Kennels howling at once was pretty grim.

Neil looked down. "So what's all this arty stuff, then?"

"It's the road to London," Chris said, squatting back and brushing hair out of his eyes, leaving a blue streak across his forehead. "You know, 'Turn again, Whittington', and all that."

The canvas showed a road and some trees, and blue sky which Chris and Hasheem were filling in. There was a signpost with *London 7* in big black letters.

"Dick makes friends with this stray dog," Chris explained. "In our case with Denny back there." He pointed to a makeshift dressing room at the side of the stage. "Then it goes to London with him and makes his fortune."

Neil wasn't really listening; Emily had been talking about the panto non-stop, and he knew the story backwards. He glanced up at the clock again. Twenty to six. "I'm going to be late," he muttered to himself.

On stage the actors and stagehands had finished moving the furniture around. Gina's older sister, Beth, came out from behind a curtain and stood centre stage. She played Dick Whittington, though she didn't look much like it at present, dressed in blue jeans and a sporty-looking hooded sweatshirt. Her long fair hair was all over the place. Denny trotted on stage as well, and sat at Beth's feet. Everybody else went off, and Neil suddenly became interested as he realized they were going to rehearse one of Denny's scenes.

Beth sat down at the table and pretended to be holding a pen. "Denny, we sold five shillings' worth of spices to Mistress Williams, and three shillings' worth to Master Snip the tailor. Five and three, Denny – what does that come to?"

Denny, who had been listening alertly, barked eight times. Neil, who knew what to look for, saw the hand signal Beth gave him when he had to stop, but it was such a small movement the audience would never notice. They would see a dog that was bright enough to do maths!

Everybody laughed and clapped when the

little scene was finished. Beth stood up and took a bow, then patted Denny. The retriever looked pleased with himself, his tongue hanging out in a wide doggy grin.

"I'm going to teach Fudge to count like that," Sarah announced.

Neil groaned.

At last, the rehearsal was coming to an end. Mr Hamley came down his ladder and Beth led Denny off stage. Everyone else began collecting their belongings and putting on their coats. Gavin Thorpe, the vicar, appeared at the door of the church hall carrying a heavy bunch of keys, ready to lock up.

"At last!" said Neil. "Can we go now?"

"What's the rush?" Hasheem asked. "You've been squirming ever since you got here."

"I've got to get home. Jake's coming tonight."

Hasheem looked puzzled. "You never said you had a mate staying for Christmas."

Chris laughed, and swiped at Hasheem with his brush. "Get real, Hasheem! Since when have you known Neil to be bothered about looking after his friends? Jake's a dog, you dimbo!"

Neil grinned at him. Chris Wilson was his best friend, and he'd heard a lot about Jake in the last few weeks. Jake was a Border collie pup – the son of Neil's beloved dog Sam, and another Border collie called Delilah, who lived at the neighbouring Old Mill Farm. Delilah had a beautiful brood of five adorable pups – and now that Jake was finally old enough to leave his mum, he was coming to live with Neil.

Delilah's owner, Jane Hammond, had promised to bring ten-week-old Jake round at six o'clock that evening. It was one appointment Neil had no intention of missing.

He said goodbye to Chris and Hasheem, and with Sarah in tow went to collect Emily, who was giggling in a corner with her friends, Gina Ward and Julie Baker. She grinned at Neil as he walked towards her.

"I told you Denny's brilliant," she said.

"That's a great scene," Neil agreed, feeling a bit disappointed that he wouldn't be in the show. "You've trained him really well, Gina."

"It's Beth really." Gina went pink with pleasure. "He'll do anything for her."

"This will be the best pantomime ever," Julie said. She laughed. "Do you think we should have Ben in it as well?"

Neil winced. Julie's Old English sheepdog, Ben, was the sloppiest and most loving dog you

9

could hope to meet – and the clumsiest. Neil smiled as he pictured flying props, furniture tipped over and scenery falling on top of a surprised but well-meaning Ben.

Then he stopped smiling. He had noticed the clock again. It said almost five to six – and where was his mother?

It was after six by the time the Parkers set off home in their green Range Rover with the King Street Kennels logo on the side. Neil was fizzing with impatience in the front seat.

"Calm down," Carole told him. "Your dad's at home. Jane will wait for you."

"But I want to be there," Neil said. "Jake's mine. I want to welcome him."

The night was already pitch black and cold and snow had started to fall. Carole was driving carefully for fear of skidding. Snowflakes whirled in the headlights. On the back seat Sarah was bouncing up and down chanting, "I'm going to make a snowman! I'm going to make a snowman!"

"Shut up, Squirt," Neil muttered.

"When are we going to decorate the tree?" Emily asked. "Can we do it tonight? Sarah and I have made some decorations."

"I made a big star," Sarah announced proudly.

"We'll see when we get home," Carole said. "We've got loads to do before Christmas, and this weather isn't helping."

Neil was feeling very excited about the thought of his new puppy. Jake would be his to look after all the time now. It wasn't just fun, Neil knew. It was a big responsibility. Just as well that school had finished, and he would have all the Christmas holiday to settle Jake into his new home.

As the Range Rover approached King Street Kennels, another car, coming from the opposite direction, turned in at the gate. Neil recognized the Hammonds' brown Volvo at once.

"There's Jane!" he exclaimed. "Brill! We haven't missed her!"

As soon as their car had stopped, Neil hurled himself into the drive and over to the Volvo where Jane Hammond was getting out. She was small and slim, with curly dark hair, and she wore a waxed jacket over a thick sweater and cord trousers.

"Hi, Neil," she said, smiling. "All ready for the new arrival?"

"Sure!" Neil grinned back.

11

Jane opened the back door of the car and reached for a pet carrier on the seat. By this time the rest of the Parkers had joined Neil.

"Is it Jake?" Sarah asked, wriggling past Neil to peer into the back of the Volvo. "Can I see?"

"Let's get him inside," Carole said. "Then we can all see."

"Don't get in the way, Squirt," Neil said. "You're holding things up. Jake will be getting cold."

Jane gave the pet carrier to Neil to carry into the house. He could feel a small body shifting around inside it and hear a scrabbling sound. Against the mesh at the front of the carrier he made out a black nose and two shining eyes.

Light flooded down the steps as the front door opened and the tall, broad-shouldered shape of Bob Parker appeared. "I thought I heard a commotion! Come inside, all of you – it's freezing out here."

Neil hurried inside with the pet carrier, squeezing past his father, and everyone crowded after him down the passage to the kitchen.

Neil set the carrier down in the middle of the kitchen floor. His fingers were shaking as he undid the strap and let the flap fall forward.

"Jake?" His voice was unsteady. "Come out, Jake. This is your new home."

A tiny black muzzle thrust itself out of the shelter of the carrier, followed by the rest of a black and white head with bright eyes and silky ears. Black paws propelled the rest of the puppy a pace or two into the kitchen where he stood watching Neil, who had squatted down in front of him.

"Jake?" Neil repeated. "Hi there, Jake."

The tiny pup looked alertly at the others who stood around him, and back at Neil. He

advanced another step and nosed at Neil's outstretched hand. His little tail suddenly began wagging frantically.

"He remembers me!" Neil said delightedly. "He knows who I am." He looked up at Jane, who stood smiling down at him. "Thanks, Jane. This really is going to be the best Christmas ever!"

Chapter Two

Sarah reached out to stroke the puppy, but Carole quickly caught her hand.

"Not just yet," she said. "Give him time to settle in first."

Jake had started to move away from the pet carrier, nose down to the kitchen floor and tail in the air as he tried to make sense of this exciting new place. Neil watched; he knew he had a silly grin on his face, and he didn't care.

"Coffee, Jane?" said Carole, above his head.

"Please. It's arctic out there, isn't it? The snow's already sticking on the lane down to the farm. That's why I was a bit late." She took out an envelope and handed it to Carole. "Before I forget, there's Jake's vaccination certificate.

He'll need a second dose in about a month, but you'll know all about that."

"I've been reading about it," Neil piped up. "If he's not vaccinated, he could get distemper and hepatitis and . . . oh, I've forgotten the others."

"Poor Jake!" said Sarah. "All those needles stuck in him!"

Bob laughed. "No, love, it's all in one injection. Though there is another vaccine against kennel cough. He'd better have that as well, because he's bound to come into contact with the boarding dogs when he's a bit older."

Neil nodded, not taking his eyes off the puppy. Whatever Jake needed to grow into a happy, healthy dog, Neil would see he had it.

As Jake was exploring the kitchen, he came close to the basket where Sam would usually be drowsing at this time. Jake sniffed the blankets inside.

As if on cue, Sam padded into the room, disturbed from his cosy spot in front of the living room fire by the noise everybody was making.

"It's Jake's dad!" Sarah clapped her hands vigorously.

Sam sat beside his basket and watched the young puppy exploring his new surroundings.

"Do you think Sam knows that he's Jake's dad?" Emily asked.

Neil held out his hand to scratch Sam's ears. "I've been reading about that, too," he explained. "Dogs don't really know about families like we do. Wild dogs live in packs, so that's how they think. Sam was here first, so he's pack leader. That means we have to show Jake that Sam's the boss."

"How do we do that?" Emily asked.

"Oh, it's easy. Feed Sam first; pat him and praise him first if they both come to you." He scratched Sam's ears again, smiling affectionately. "Jake's terrific, but Sam mustn't feel left out."

Sam had been Neil's dog for years, ever since he had been found as a puppy, abandoned and wandering on the old Compton railway line. Until recently, he had been a champion in local Agility competitions. But just a few weeks ago, at the same time Jake was born, they had discovered that Sam had a heart murmur. Even though he was still a happy, healthy dog, there would be no more Agility contests for Sam. He had to take it easy from now on.

Neil laughed as Jake put his paws up on the edge of the basket and sniffed curiously at Sam.

Sam bent his head; father and son touched nose to nose.

"Aren't they sweet!" said Emily.

"Hey!" Neil said as Jake's hind feet scrabbled against the basket. The pup was trying to climb in, and Neil wasn't sure how Sam would take the invading of his territory.

Neil gently pushed Jake away. Carefully he picked him up with one hand under his chest and the other supporting his hindquarters, and carried him across the kitchen.

"This is your basket, Jake," he said.

For now, Neil had brought in one of the plastic beds that they used in the rescue centre, and padded it with warm bedding. Puppies always chew their beds, and letting Jake chew a proper basket might hurt him when he was so tiny.

Next to the bed were two big china bowls. Neil put Jake down in front of them and filled one of them with water. Jake stuck his nose in for a long drink.

"Isn't he small?" Sarah said.

"Biggest in the litter!" Neil protested.

"He's very young," Carole explained to Sarah. "But he'll grow. You just wait!"

Sarah gazed at Jake as if she expected him to

grow in front of her eyes. "Aren't you going to feed him?" she asked.

"Give him a small meal later on," Jane suggested. "He's on four meals a day at the moment: two of puppy meal with milk, and two of mince mixed with brown bread – cornflakes now and again for a change. I've been putting a teaspoonful of bonemeal and one of cod liver oil in one of the meat meals."

Neil nodded, taking it all in.

"I've brought some of the puppy meal we've been using," Jane went on. "You can change to your own once he's settled in."

Sarah was still watching Jake as he drank. "I'd like a puppy for Christmas," she said.

"You're always wanting a puppy!" laughed Neil.

"You're too young to look after a puppy on your own yet," Carole explained. "But I'm sure Neil would like some help with Jake once he's settled in."

"You're just a pup yourself, Squirt!" said Emily.

Neil didn't say anything.

"Besides," said Bob, "remember that a puppy's for life, not just for Christmas." Every year the Parkers had to find new homes for pups who'd been given as Christmas presents and then abandoned by owners who couldn't cope. People just didn't realize what a responsibility a puppy could be.

As Jake finished his drink Carole said to Neil, "You should really take him outside after that. But it's so cold I've put some newspaper down by the door. Use that for now. Just lift him over there and see if he gets the idea."

Neil did as his mother suggested, but Jake immediately bounced off the newspaper again. Neil put him back. Jake gave him a look as if he wanted to say, "What's all this about?" but after a minute he squatted down and produced the expected puddle.

"Well done, boy! Good dog!" Neil praised him, while Sarah jumped up and down and clapped as if the pup had done something clever. Maybe he had; it was better than in the middle of the floor. All the same, Neil thought, as he collected up the soggy newspaper, he'd be *much* happier when it was warm enough for Jake to go outside.

When Neil went down to breakfast next morning, Jake was romping round the kitchen.

After feeding Sam and then the puppy, he sat down for his own breakfast just as Bob Parker came in through the back door in a swirl of fluffy snow.

"Shut the door, Dad!" cried Emily, already seated at the table. "You're letting the warm air out."

"Yeah, and think of Jake! He'll catch a chill!" Neil warned, pouring himself a bowl of cereal.

The puppy danced around Bob's wellington boots, sniffing the sludgy snow as it fell to the floor and seeming oblivious to the icy blast.

Bob unzipped his thick winter jacket and stomped his feet on the floormat. He nudged Jake back towards his basket. "Sorry, but it's absolutely freezing out there – I had to come inside again for a moment to get warmed up. I've been chipping the ice off the barn doors. They're getting almost impossible to open."

Neil looked up. "Is it that bad?"

"Worst I've seen for a long time. Make sure you've got proper boots on if you go out. The snow is already fairly deep between here and the kennel blocks. I hope it doesn't go on too much longer or we'll have trouble keeping things running."

Emily laughed and pointed towards a pile of

post on the table. "Anyway, if the mail's still being delivered it can't be that bad!"

Neil flicked through the pile. Most of the letters were for Bob and Carole, but there was a copy of the animal magazine that Emily subscribed to, and one large white envelope for him. Neil ripped it open.

"Hey, great," he said. "Look, it's a card from Max and Prince." Quickly he read the few lines scribbled inside the card. "Max says they're recording up here again in the New Year. He might be able to drop in and see us."

Max Hooper, with his dog Prince, was the star of the Parkers' favourite TV programme, *Time Travellers*, and not long ago, Neil and Emily had been extras in an episode recorded at Padsham Castle. Neil and Max had kept in touch ever since, and Neil was delighted at the thought of seeing his friend again. He was sure Max and Prince would love to meet Jake.

Carole had served up eggs and bacon, and was now looking through her own cards.

"One from Mr Bradshaw and Marjorie," she said, passing it over to Bob. "And one from Eddie and Maureen Thomas, and Blackie – look at the paw-print! And a calendar from Preston's – Bob, that reminds me. Did you check up when they'll deliver the dog food I ordered in for the holidays? We'll be needing it before long."

Bob swallowed a mouthful of bacon. "I rang them yesterday. They've got problems fitting in all the deliveries before Christmas, but they promised me it would be here by tomorrow at the latest."

"I'll believe it when I see it," Carole said.

After breakfast, Neil got ready to help with the kennel work.

"Don't forget to wrap up warm," said Carole. "The snow didn't let up overnight."

When Neil opened the back door he saw the courtyard covered with a layer of white, already criss-crossed by lines of footprints from the kennel blocks to the house, the barn, and the separate block that housed the rescue centre. Thin, wispy flakes of snow fluttered down and swirled all round.

Neil pulled down his hat over his ears, and launched himself into the snow.

In the store room he found Kate McGuire, the King Street kennel maid, measuring out the feeds for the boarding dogs. Her fair hair was tied back, and she was wearing some thin thermal gloves.

"Hi!" Neil said. "Jane brought Jake round last night. Are you coming to see him?"

"You bet," Kate said. "Just as soon as I've finished here. This is the last batch." She dug the scoop deep into the sack of biscuits. "We're running low. I hope we get that delivery before Christmas."

"Tomorrow, Dad said," Neil told her. "Do you want me to take these in?" He nodded towards the bowls.

King Street Kennels had two kennel blocks, with the store room between them. Each of the blocks had two rows of ten pens, with an aisle down the middle, and each pen had its own separate exercise run. Today, though, the doors to the runs were closed, to keep out the cold.

As Neil opened the door of Kennel Block Two, a blast of warm air greeted him. The blocks were heated during the colder weather by pipes running through the concrete floor; his dad must have turned the heating right up.

The frantic barking of the last few hungry dogs sank to a contented snuffling as they pushed their noses into their bowls. With the job done, Neil took a few minutes to talk to the dogs. Some of them had been regular visitors to King Street for years.

"Hello there, Bundle," he said, stopping in front of a hairy mongrel who had spent some time in the rescue centre. The last time Bundle was at King Street, he'd been bright pink – the result of a cruel practical joke. "You're looking well."

He slipped Bundle a dog treat from the supply he always carried in his pocket. Next to Bundle was Flora, a Jack Russell who was a regular visitor, and next to her a Welsh corgi called Taffy.

The pen at the far end of the block had been empty when Neil went out the day before. Now it was occupied. Neil peered in to see one of the biggest dogs he'd ever seen, sitting and looking back at him with a sorrowful expression in his liquid brown eyes. The dog had a shaggy brown and white coat, with a white muzzle and chest, and black shading on his face and ears.

"A St Bernard!" Neil exclaimed. "Wow, you're massive, aren't you?" He held out a titbit through the mesh, half afraid that the enormous dog would swallow his fingers as well.

Neil heard Kate's footsteps approaching him down the aisle.

"What's his name, Kate?" asked Neil.

"Bernie. His owner left him here yesterday, while he goes off to Spain for some winter sun." She flicked some snowflakes off her shoulders. "Can't say I blame him."

"But it's warm in here. Anyway, if one of us gets lost in the snow, Bernie can come and find us."

Kate laughed. "Don't bet on it. His owner, John Cartwright, used to train dogs for the mountain rescue service, before he retired. He told me that Bernie was the only dog he'd never been able to train at all."

Neil stared at the St Bernard again. "He's never saved anybody?"

"Not one."

Huh, Neil thought, *I bet I could train him!* Then he stopped himself. He mustn't get too big-headed. John Cartwright was a professional, after all, and if he couldn't train Bernie . . . Neil gave the big dog a last glance as he followed the others out of the kennel block. *All the same,* he thought, *I'd like to have a try.*

As Neil crossed the courtyard again, blowing warm air into his gloved hands, he glanced through the side gate and saw a blue Mini turn into the drive. The car glided silently to a halt on the deepening snow and Gina Ward scrambled out almost before it had stopped. Neil walked over to meet her.

"Hi," he said. "Have you come to—"

He broke off, noticing her tears. "Neil, it's awful!" she said. "We've lost Denny!"

Chapter Three

"Lost Denny?" Neil echoed. "What do you mean? How?"

"I don't know." Gina twisted the ends of her scarf worriedly. She looked very upset. "He went out in the garden this morning, and when I went to call him in, he'd gone!"

"Are you sure he isn't hiding?"

While they were talking, Gina's sister Beth had got out of the driver's seat and come to join them.

"Have you seen our garden, Neil?" she asked. "A mouse couldn't hide in there, never mind a dog the size of Denny. I found a loose post in the fence; I think he must have squeezed out that way."

"Have you tried following his paw marks in the snow?" Neil suggested.

Gina shook her head. "It wasn't any good. We could see his prints in the garden, but too many people had been up and down the lane outside." Gina looked up at the white snowflakes drifting down all round them. "Maybe the snow confused him. It's the first time he's seen it settle so deeply. Everything looks so different – even our garden."

"I rang the police," Beth said, "but they haven't heard anything yet. They suggested getting in touch with your dad."

That didn't surprise Neil. Stray dogs in and around Compton often ended up at the King Street rescue centre. Neil had lost count of how many frantic owners the Parkers had reunited with their pets. He knew how Gina and Beth must be feeling but there was nothing he could do to help them – Denny wasn't here.

"I'm sorry," he said, "but we've not heard anything, either."

Beth shook her head. "I didn't expect you would have, really. I know you would have rung us. But we had to give it a try. You will get in touch if he turns up?"

"Of course we will. You'd better come and

give his details to Mum. And let's get inside – it's freezing standing here."

Neil led Beth and Gina to the office. Emily had seen the car from the house, and ran to meet them at the door. She was shocked to hear that Denny was missing.

"What about the pantomime?" she asked. "We can't do it without Denny. He's too important!"

"I know," said Beth. "And he's usually so good. I can't help thinking something horrible has happened."

Carole looked up from her desk. "Don't say that. It's early days yet. Let's not jump to conclusions, eh?" She sat Gina and Beth down in front of the desk and began to record Denny's details for the rescue centre files. Neil and Emily crowded round to listen.

"He was definitely wearing his collar," Gina said. "It has a tag with his name and our phone number. So if someone *has* found him, why haven't they let us know? Only a thief wouldn't call."

"I know this is horrible for you, but you've got to keep calm," Carole said. "He's only been missing two or three hours and it doesn't do any good to think the worst."

Neil exchanged a worried glance with Emily. Denny was such a clever dog, and so well-trained, that if a thief knew about him he might think he could sell him for a good price.

"Have you seen anybody suspicious hanging around?" he asked.

Beth looked blank, and said that as far as she could recall there was nobody in the lane when she let Denny into the garden that morning.

"Tell them about that phone call," said Gina, nudging her sister's arm.

Beth nodded. "Just two or three days ago I had an anonymous phone call. It was a man. He sounded very reasonable at first – asking me lots of questions about the pantomime. Eventually he claimed we were being cruel to Denny by teaching him tricks and making him perform. He asked me not to use him in the show."

"Huh!" Emily snorted. "You don't have to *make* Denny perform. He loves it!"

"What did you say?" Neil asked.

"Nothing. I just put the phone down."

"And did you tell the police?" Carole made a note on the card where she was recording Denny's details.

31

"No." Beth shrugged. "I thought it was just some crank. But now I wonder whether he came and stole Denny to stop him being in the pantomime."

Everybody was silent for a minute. Neil knew that some trainers were cruel to performing animals, and some kinds of animal were unhappy in captivity, but none of that applied to Denny. He was a happy, healthy dog, and Neil had seen at the rehearsal how he loved to show off. Even so, somebody who didn't know him might think he was rescuing him from ill-treatment.

"I think you should report it to the police now," said Carole.

"Yes, I will." Beth glanced at her watch. "Come on, Gina. Emily, I'll see you later on at rehearsal."

"But will we be doing the pantomime, if Denny can't be found?" Emily protested.

"I don't know. But we can still rehearse. There are lots of scenes that Denny isn't in." She gave Emily a little shake, and managed to smile. "Cheer up, Emily. The show must go on!"

"I've worked out a training programme for Bernie," Neil announced at lunchtime. He sat at the kitchen table, carefully avoiding Jake, who was making little growly rushes at his feet.

"For Bernie?" Bob Parker gave his spaghetti sauce on the cooker a last stir. "I thought you had enough to do, training Jake."

Neil felt himself going red. "Yes, well . . . I thought it would be a surprise for Mr Cartwright."

"John Cartwright has been training dogs for years," Carole pointed out. "If he says Bernie is untrainable . . ."

"But there's no harm in trying," Neil said. "Em, you'll help me, won't you?"

Emily sat down, and pushed her untidy dark hair out of her eyes.

"Not now. I've got a rehearsal. If I've got time later I might give you a hand."

"Sarah?" Asking for his little sister's help was a last resort for Neil – but probably better than nothing.

"I'm going to build a snowman!" Sarah said. "Fudge is going to help me."

"Thanks a bunch," Neil muttered. He was beginning to think that his attempt at training Bernie would have to wait.

"It's too cold for Fudge to be outside," Carole said, as she began serving out the sauce. "But

Neil's very good at building snowmen." She gave Neil a hard look. "Aren't you, Neil?"

Neil shrugged. "Oh, sure."

Bob chuckled. "And don't be too disappointed if Bernie doesn't co-operate when you do get a chance to take him out. I don't think snow and Bernie get along very well together!"

When Emily had gone to her rehearsal, Neil helped Sarah to build a snowman in the courtyard during a break in the weather. He rolled a huge snowball for the body while Sarah made a smaller one for the head. She fetched an old hat and a scarf, while Neil raided the storeroom for biscuits to make eyes, a nose and mouth.

Neil bent down and plunged his hand deep into a large, brown sack. Scrabbling round at the bottom, he pulled out a handful of dog biscuits and stuffed them in his jacket pocket. On his way out, he noticed that they really were getting low on dog food – there was probably only enough to last a couple of days.

When he went back into the courtyard he found Sarah rolling a third snowball.

"Not another snowman!" he protested. "I'm

freezing. And it's getting harder to walk in this stuff!" Neil kicked out at a lump of snow on the ground.

"No, stupid," Sarah said. "This is a snow dog!"

They finished off the snow dog with a curved twig for a tail and Sarah's scarf around its neck. She didn't want it getting cold. It didn't look like any breed of dog Neil had ever seen. Just as they had completed their snow sculpture, it started to snow again, big wet flakes that settled on the window ledge and the ground and the roofs of the kennel blocks. They had to leave the snowman and his dog, and take shelter. If the snow got much deeper, Neil thought, they might get cut off for Christmas.

As Neil went into the kitchen, something tiny collided with his foot. He looked down to see Jake trying to attack his boot. Jake was into feet. If you were that small, Neil thought, feet might be the most important thing you could see.

Grinning, he squatted down and tickled the little black and white pup on the tummy. "What about some training, Jake?"

Neil started by calling Sam over from his

basket. The Border collie came promptly and stood looking at Neil with an alert expression.

"Now watch this," Neil said to Jake. He took out a dog treat, showed it to Sam, and said, "Sit!" Sam sat at once; Neil gave him the treat and praised him. "Now, Jake, do you think you can do that?"

Jake had watched with an interested look in his bright eyes, but as soon as Neil took out

another titbit he started bouncing around, trying to reach his hand.

"No!" said Neil.

He held out the dog treat to Jake, who sniffed it while his little tail wagged excitedly. Neil lifted the titbit above his head, and Jake sat down to keep his eyes on it more easily. He gave Jake the titbit and fondled his ears as the puppy wolfed it down.

Looking at Jake, Neil thought about Beth and Gina, who must have been missing Denny desperately. He wished he could do something to help. It would be a miserable Christmas for the Ward family without Denny.

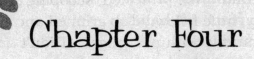

Chapter Four

Neil knew how right he was when his dad brought Emily back from rehearsal. She was almost in tears.

"It was awful. Everybody was upset, trying to work without Denny. And Gina's really worried because Denny might freeze to death if he's out all night in this snow."

"It almost makes you hope he has been stolen," Bob said, taking his coat off. "At least a thief would keep him inside. It'll be bitter outside tonight. If the snow keeps lying like it has been doing I can see problems ahead."

He shook the melting remains of snow off his coat. Jake flinched and his paws skittered on the floor as one of the flying drops hit him.

"Hey Dad!" Neil protested, scooping Jake up.

"Sorry, little fellow." Bob grinned and rubbed Jake's muzzle with one finger. "Didn't see you down there."

"Maybe one of the dogs could track Denny," Emily suggested, cheering up a bit. "Perhaps Bernie could do it."

"Not yet – I haven't worked my magic on him!"

"Modesty is not your strong point, is it?" Emily tried to hide a smile. "I think Jake could do a better job of tracking than Bernie."

Bob was still stroking the pup in Neil's arms. "Somehow I don't think so." He smiled gently down at Jake. "He's got a lot of learning to do first."

Just then Carole and Kate opened the back door and bustled into the warmth of the kitchen. Carole's hands were filled with holly, covered in shiny scarlet berries. She laid it carefully on the table, then unwound her scarf and pulled off her woolly hat.

"It's cold enough out there to freeze your feet off," she said. "Is there a hot drink on offer, Bob?"

Bob hurriedly went to the sink to fill the kettle. Kate stripped off her gloves and blew on fingers turned pink with cold.

"It's at times like this," she said, "that I fancy a job in a nice, warm office."

"No!" Emily protested. "You can't!"

Kate laughed. "I was only joking. I don't really. But the snow's getting worse. We'll need skis to get across the courtyard tomorrow."

Neil looked out of the window again. A white veil of snowflakes whirled against the darkening sky.

"Maybe we'll be snowed in," he suggested. "That would be ace!"

His mother gave him one of her looks. "If we are, you'll soon be wishing I'd shopped for more food. Feeding you lot is like feeding an army on the march. Not to mention the dogs!"

Bob poured coffee into mugs and handed one to Kate. "You're never going to be able to ride your bike home in this."

Kate wrapped her hands gratefully round the steaming mug. "No need to worry. Glen said he would collect me."

"Good," said Bob. "And I really don't think you should try to come in tomorrow."

"But the dogs still have to be looked after," Kate objected. "It's harder work when the weather's like this."

Bob shrugged. "We'll cope. But if it keeps on

snowing, you might not be able to get here. And if you do, you might not be able to get home again. That would really mess up your plans for Christmas."

"What are you doing for Christmas, Kate?" Emily asked.

"Spending it with Glen, of course," said Neil, grinning. "Look, she's gone bright red!"

"Neil!" said his mother.

Just then the doorbell rang. Emily went to answer it, and came back with Kate's boyfriend, Glen Paget, his collar turned up and his long, fair hair plastered to his head with melting snow. He said hello to everyone, and scratched Jake behind the ears. "Hi there, midget. I've heard a lot about you."

"Listen, Glen," Carole said, "tell Kate that she's not to try coming into work tomorrow. The snow's getting worse. It's not worth risking an accident."

"She's right, you know," Glen said to Kate. "It was hard enough getting here tonight."

Kate looked from Carole to Bob, and then back at Glen. Reluctantly, she nodded. "All right."

"And don't look so guilty," Bob told her. "Have an extra day's holiday on the Puppy Patrol."

"And this," added Carole, taking a parcel in shiny paper out of a cupboard and presenting it to Kate.

Kate hugged it to her and thanked them. "I'm really sorry. I just hope you have a good Christmas."

"We will," Bob said. "And you enjoy yours, too."

"I'll make sure she does," Glen promised cheerfully.

As Kate and Glen were about to leave, Neil thought about Denny. Glen was involved with an Animal Rights group, and he might be able to shed some light on the crank phone call Beth had received.

"Glen," he asked, "do you know the Wards' dog, Denny?"

Glen shook his head. Quickly Neil explained about Denny's cleverness, and how someone had phoned to tell Beth she was cruel to make the dog perform. "And now Denny's missing," he finished. "Do you know of anyone who might have taken him?"

"To keep him out of the pantomime?" Glen thought for a minute. "That's a tough one, Neil. Some people don't like to see performing animals, but a trained pet dog is different from lions and tigers that should be in the wild. I can tell you this, nobody in my group would steal a dog. I doubt that it's anything to do with Animal Rights."

"It doesn't sound as if Denny was stolen," Neil said when Glen and Kate had gone. He almost felt disappointed. At least an Animal Rights group would look after Denny.

"So he might be wandering about in the snow," said Emily, gloomy again. "And they've cancelled tomorrow's rehearsal. If someone doesn't find Denny soon, there won't be any pantomime."

In the excitement of Jake's arrival the night before, they'd forgotten the Christmas tree. Neil, Emily and Sarah decorated it in the sitting room after supper. Sarah insisted on Bob lifting her up so that she could put the glittery star she had made on the topmost branch. Carole kept the fragile baubles out of Jake's reach, but the excitable little puppy still managed to roll himself up in tinsel.

"He's so sweet!" said Emily.

Carole was on her knees disguising the very ordinary bucket that held the tree with shiny Christmas paper. She stopped what she was doing to unwind Jake.

"You'll have to keep an eye on him, Neil," she said. "I hate to think what he would do if you left him in here by himself."

"Sure, Mum." Neil grinned, and scooped Jake up to pick the last strand of tinsel out of his glossy coat. "Behave yourself, Jake, do you hear? And make sure you don't scare Father Christmas!"

"I think we should write to Father Christmas and ask him to bring Denny back," Sarah announced.

"You've left it a bit late," Emily said.

"Well, I'm going to!"

"You write if you want to, love," Carole said. "The Wards couldn't hope for a better Christmas present, that's for sure."

*

On Christmas Eve morning Neil woke early. He looked out to see the courtyard and the roofs of the kennel blocks covered with snow. There had been another heavy snowfall during the night, but now only a few flakes were drifting slowly down. The bedroom window was covered with frost patterns, and icicles hung from the gutter above.

The rest of the house was quiet. It would be a good time for a training session with Bernie. Neil would have to manage without a helper, but at least there would be no one there to laugh at him.

He washed quickly, and dragged on jeans and a couple of thick sweaters, wondering what he could use to lay a trail of scent for Bernie. Then he had an idea.

He took the pillowcase from his pillow, fished out some abandoned socks from under the bed and put them in the case, then topped it up with a couple of his shirts, a sweater and some more socks from the laundry basket. That lot should have plenty of his scent on them. Satisfied, he tied a knot in the top of the pillowcase and crept downstairs.

When he got down to the kitchen, Jake was asleep, but Sam lifted his head alertly from his basket.

"No, Sam," Neil said. "Not now. It's far too cold for you outside."

When he had put on his boots and padded jacket, Neil took his bundle outside into the exercise field. On one side of the field the powdery snow had drifted so that it came almost to the top of his boots, and his breath made a cloud in the icy morning air. Starting near the gate, he dragged the bundle through the snow where it wasn't too deep, back and forth for a long way, and finally buried it.

"Right," he said to himself. "Let's see what he makes of that."

Neil opened the door of Kennel Block Two a crack, and slid quietly inside. He didn't want to wake all the dogs; the racket would wake everyone else, and his mum and dad would be furious.

The air inside the block was warm, and the dogs were mostly still asleep. One or two raised their heads drowsily and watched Neil as he padded along the aisle between the pens.

When he reached Bernie's pen, Neil took the lead from the hook outside the door and went in. Bernie was snoring in a regular rumble that shook his whole body. Neil bent down and tugged at his collar.

"Come on, boy! Wake up!"

Bernie opened one liquid eye and closed it again. His snores died away into a kind of hiccup, and then started up again. Neil gave him a gentle shove.

"Come *on!*"

This time Bernie woke up properly, thrust himself to his feet and gave himself a shake. Neil grinned and slipped him a dog treat.

"That's better. Let's go, Bernie!"

As Neil led Bernie outside he heard a high-pitched yapping from the Pomeranian in the nearest pen, and Bundle's deeper bark answering it from further down the row. *Go back to sleep,* he willed them silently, leading Bernie at a trot down the garden path and through the gate.

Once in the exercise field, Neil forgot about the other dogs. Pulling out one of his socks that he'd stashed in his pocket, Neil waved it under Bernie's nostrils. The dog's nostrils flared as he sniffed it. Neil then unclipped Bernie's lead and let him nose around in the snow, trying to encourage him to find the end of the scent trail he had laid.

When Bernie reached it, he became quite excited, snuffling around with his nose in Neil's footprints.

Neil crouched down beside him. "Seek, Bernie!"

Bernie nosed around again, and at last came back to Neil and planted a huge, snow-covered paw on his chest. Neil staggered back, laughing.

"No, you daft dog! Other end . . . seek!"

Somehow, Bernie seemed to grasp the idea. He plodded back and forth along the scent trail, until he reached the pillowcase that Neil had buried, and scraped energetically at the snow to uncover it.

Neil stooped over him and gave him a big hug. "Brill, Bernie! Well done!"

He fed Bernie a couple of dog treats, and decided he would end the training session there. Next time, Bernie would remember he had done well. If I play with him for a bit, Neil thought, he'll want to try again.

They had ended up near the clump of bushes at the far end of the field. Neil found a stick, and threw it for Bernie. The huge dog lolloped back and forth, scattering snow everywhere, enjoying the game just as if he were a pup like Jake.

Neil only remembered the time when snow started to fall again. It soon came down in multiple sheets of tingly, wet drops and Neil quickly called Bernie back to him.

"Breakfast, Bernie?"

He was sure the St Bernard grinned at him. He clipped on the lead again and tried to lead him away but instead Bernie sat rock-like, and gave a yawn. Neil tugged the lead gently, and when Bernie still did not respond he hauled on the St Bernard's collar. It was like trying to shift a cart-horse. "Up, Bernie! Come on! Just for me?" Neil beamed at the dog. "Please?"

At last Bernie heaved himself to his feet and trundled off up the field, with Neil striding alongside him, picking up the pillowcase as he went. As soon as Bernie reached the gate, he flopped to the ground again.

Neil swung open the gate and motioned for Bernie to go through.

Bernie dropped his nose to his paws looking completely uninterested.

"I don't often beg, Bernie, but will you please come back to the kennels with me? The snow is going down my neck!"

The St Bernard's head swivelled to look at Neil, and then with a ripple of muscles he rose and plodded back towards the kennels. Already the snow was so heavy that he could hardly see the shape of the house and the kennel blocks, but as he drew closer, he could make out the figure of his father coming towards him across the courtyard. Neil broke into a run, with Bernie alongside him.

"Dad!" he panted, as he reached him. "You'll never guess what Bernie . . ."

His voice died away as he saw his father's face. Bob Parker was hardly ever angry, but he looked angry now.

"Neil," he said, "what exactly have you been doing?"

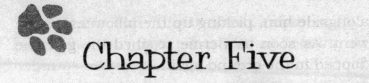

Chapter Five

"Sorry?" Neil said, staring up into his father's face.

"I hope you are." Bob still sounded grim. He motioned for Neil to follow him across the courtyard. "Your mother and I were woken up at some unearthly hour by all the dogs barking their heads off—"

"Oops," said Neil.

"When we found out that Bernie was missing from his pen, the first thing we thought was that somebody must have broken into the kennels. Then your mother looked into your room, and found you were missing as well."

"I'm sorry, Dad. I just thought it was a good chance to give Bernie a bit of training. And he—"

51

"You didn't think at all," Bob interrupted. He stopped as they came to the door of Kennel Block One; when he spoke again he sounded less angry. "Neil, I know you meant it for the best. But your mum and I have got enough to do today, especially when Kate isn't here, without having to look for a missing dog that isn't missing at all. I was within a couple of minutes of ringing the police. Go and put Bernie back in his pen right now. And Neil . . . try to be a bit more sensible in future."

When Neil had kennelled Bernie he went back to the house and found the rest of the family having breakfast round the kitchen table. Sam and Jake were both looking on hopefully. Neil stamped snow off his boots.

"That smells good," he said, sniffing appreciatively as Carole dished up sausages and bacon.

"Think yourself lucky that I didn't give yours to Jake," Carole said. "Sit down and . . . Neil – what in the world is *that*?"

Neil was still carrying the pillowcase full of clothes that he had used to lay the scent trail for Bernie.

"It's just clothes and stuff," he explained. "I used it to—"

"If you ask me, you've been playing football with it!" Carol said. "Neil, just look at it! That was a good pillowcase."

Neil looked at his bundle properly for the first time since Bernie had dug it up. He had to admit it was filthy, and it had got torn a bit. Still, in Neil's view, it was worth it if it had helped to train Bernie.

"You see, Mum—"

"I don't want to know." Carole sounded exasperated. "I really don't. Just take it up to the laundry basket, and then come and have your breakfast."

The snow went on falling. By the time breakfast was over, the footprints Neil and his dad had made in the courtyard were filled in again.

"I'm glad I finished the Christmas shopping," Carole said, as she cleared the table. "I wouldn't fancy driving in this."

Bob got up, nodding at Neil and Emily. "Come on, you two. Feeding time."

Without Kate, it took longer than usual to make up the feeds for the boarding dogs. Bob measured out the different diets, while Neil and

Emily transported the bowls of food and water to the two kennel blocks and the rescue centre. Carole stayed indoors to get on with Christmas preparations.

"To think I ever wanted snow!" Neil groaned, slipping and narrowly saving the food bowl he was carrying. Even in gloves his fingers felt like icicles. The falling snow was so intense he could hardly see across the courtyard. He couldn't help wondering what would happen to Denny, if he was out in this. There had been no word from Beth or Gina since the day before and Neil could imagine how they must be feeling.

When the feeding was done, Neil and Emily went back into the kitchen, where Carole had hot drinks ready. A tray of mince pies had appeared on the kitchen table. Neil reached for one.

"Hands off!" Carole swatted him. "They're for tomorrow."

"Quality control, Mum," Neil protested.

To avoid any more arguments, Carole put a packet of chocolate biscuits on the table. "Is there any sign of the dog food?" she asked Bob.

"No. I'm starting to wonder if the delivery van will be able to get through. I'm going to give

Preston's a ring." Bob drained his mug and went out into the hall.

Emily said, "Is there any news of Denny?"

Carole shook her head. "I'd have told you if there was. Try not to worry, love. He might have found shelter somewhere."

She meant to be comforting, but she still sounded anxious. Everybody knew the danger Denny was in. Even watching Jake's antics as he tried to chase his own tail couldn't cheer Neil up. And he couldn't think of anything more that they could do.

When Bob came back, he was looking worried as well, but for a different reason.

"I got through to the delivery manager, and he told me the snow had messed up all their schedules. Only to be expected, I suppose. He said he'd try to get a van through to us, but he couldn't promise."

"Well," Carole said, "we've food for a couple of days. Let's see . . ." She started counting on her fingers. "Today's Thursday. Christmas Day and Boxing Day . . . Bob, if they don't deliver today, there won't be another delivery until next Monday."

"What are we going to do?" asked Neil.

"There's the Cash and Carry on the other side

of Compton," Carole said. "It'll be expensive but we could buy some cases of tinned dog food there, and biscuits."

"Getting there's the problem," said Bob. He straightened up. "Let's leave it until lunch time. Then we'll decide. Neil, come and help me clear the drive so we can get the car out, and if the Preston's van arrives, it can get in."

By the end of the morning, Neil's back was aching from shovelling snow and he was sweating inside his padded jacket. More snow was falling all the time, so he couldn't help feeling that all his efforts would be wasted. But he and his father had cleared a path from the road to the house, and Bob had put down some of the straw that was used for the dogs' bedding, to help wheels get a grip.

"If the snow stops," Bob said, "we'll clear some of the exercise runs. That way the dogs can get out for a bit."

"Fantastic," Neil grunted. He never wanted to see another spade for the rest of his life. "Can we go in now? I've still got to wrap presents."

"Better do it later," Bob suggested. "When Sarah's in bed. She won't give you a minute's peace, otherwise."

Neil grinned.

Neil and Bob took the spades back to the store room. On the way, they met Emily and Sarah, plodding back through the snow from the rescue centre.

"We've been checking up on the dogs," Emily explained. "They're really restless because they haven't been out. We played with them for a bit but Sarah wanted to play with Jake."

"Look for her Christmas presents, more like," Neil smirked.

"We'll try to get them out this afternoon," Bob promised. "Otherwise there'll be a lot of very messy pens to clean out."

Emily made a face. "There already are!"

Carole was in the store room when Neil and Bob put away the spades.

"I've made a list," she explained, waving it. "Of what we really can't do without. If Preston's don't turn up, I'll go to the Cash and Carry after lunch."

Mention of lunch reminded Neil that he was starving. He led the way across the courtyard to the house. Halfway there, he was met by Sam, padding through the snow and waving his tail cheerfully.

"Oh, Sam!" Neil exclaimed. "Don't say you've

learnt how to open the back door!"

He was leading Sam back indoors when a dreadful thought struck him. Where was Jake? He hurried on ahead into the kitchen. It was empty. Though Neil looked under the table and in the spaces behind the fridge and the cooker, there was no sign of the vulnerable little puppy.

Neil dashed out into the passage.

"Jake! Jake!" he called anxiously into the emptiness.

No little puppy scurried up to answer him. Everything was quiet. Neil quickly checked the sitting room, the dining room they hardly ever used, the cloakroom and the cupboard under the stairs. Nothing. Emily tried to ask him what he was up to but he rushed past her into the kitchen without answering.

"Jake! Jake, where are you?"

Carole caught up with Neil first. She took one look at his panic-stricken face and asked, "Neil! What on earth is wrong?"

"Mum! Dad!" Neil gasped out frantically, resisting their efforts to calm him. "Jake's missing. I can't find him anywhere!"

Chapter Six

"Steady on," Bob said. "He must be around here somewhere."

"I've looked," Neil said. "He must have got out. I think Sam opened the back door."

"I doubt even Sam's clever enough for that," said Carole. "But one of us might not have shut it properly."

"Jake loves exploring," Emily said worriedly.

Neil headed for the door. "He'll freeze out there!"

"Hang on," said Bob. "Let's make sure he isn't here, first."

"I said, I've looked."

"So let's look again."

59

Neil felt frustrated at the methodical way his father started checking the downstairs rooms again, and then went upstairs, even though Jake hadn't learnt to climb stairs yet.

Neil ran outside into the courtyard with Emily. He looked at the ground to see if he could find pawprints leading away from the back door – but a busy morning of people tramping back and forth through the snow made it difficult to see anything clearly. Any marks there were which might have been tiny pawprints were rapidly filling up with snow. It was useless.

"Where do you think he'd go?" Emily asked.

"I don't know. He's not really been out yet. He hasn't got any favourite places."

Neil and Emily began to search the courtyard, calling for Jake all the time. Neil was frightened that the puppy might have got out onto the road, but he realized that was unlikely. He would have seen Jake if the pup had come out while he and his father were shovelling snow in the drive, and they had closed the side gate carefully when they had finished.

The doors of the kennel blocks and the rescue centre were all firmly closed to keep the heat in. Red's Barn was closed as well, but Bob had been in and out fetching straw, and Jake could have slipped in then. Neil and Emily searched.

The barn was a wonderful place for a little dog to play and hide, but after a few minutes they were sure Jake was not there either.

When they left the barn they saw Bob coming out into the courtyard. "Any luck?" he called over to them.

"No," said Neil. "Let's try the garden."

All the while Neil was trying to push down the sick feeling in his stomach, desperately hoping that he would see the little black and white Border collie come bounding towards him through the snow. He wondered how long Jake had been outside. He would freeze to death if they didn't find him soon.

There was still no sign of Jake when he and Bob and Emily came to the field gate. Through the swirling snow Neil could just make out the hedge that separated their land from the Hammonds'.

"Do you think Jake tried to go home?" he asked Bob.

"To Old Mill Farm? I doubt it. Jane delivered him here by road. He wouldn't know the way across the fields."

"We could ring Jane, though," Neil suggested.

"She'll ring us if Jake turns up. I don't want to worry her. Not yet, anyway."

Emily pushed open the gate into the field. "He could have come through here. Sam used to get through the hedge when he went to visit Delilah. Let's start looking."

Neil bit back a groan. The field was huge! If Jake was wandering round, they could easily miss him in the snow. The idea crossed his mind that he might get Bernie to track Jake, but he had to face up to the fact that he hadn't made any real progress with the dopey St Bernard. Not enough to risk Jake's life to his tracking skills.

Neil started calling again, working his way alongside the hedge, poking into the bushes with a stick to see if Jake was hiding. Snow spattered from the branches to the ground as he disturbed them, but there was no Jake.

Eventually he reached the clump of trees and bushes at the far end of the field.

"Jake! Jake!"

For a few seconds he heard nothing except his own panting breath. Then he thought that he could make out a faint whimpering. Emily came pounding up, skidded to a halt beside him and grabbed his arm.

"Call again."

"Jake!"

This time Neil was certain. Jake had answered him. He plunged into the undergrowth, dislodging great masses of snow that slithered wetly onto his shoulders. Neil didn't notice. As he called Jake, the pup's reply had become a feeble yapping.

Neil found him at last in front of a huge clump of brambles several feet from the fence. Trailing stems arched over, interlaced so they protected the ground underneath from some of the snow. He pushed back the curtain with one gloved hand. Beneath it, Jake was crouched on

a carpet of snow and dead leaves. When Neil appeared he got up, staggered a couple of paces to sniff Neil's hand, and then collapsed again, shivering. Neil gathered him up.

"Oh, Jake!" He was swallowing tears; he told himself that was stupid, now that Jake was found. "Jake, you daft dog. What have you been up to?"

Back in the kitchen, Neil wrapped Jake in a blanket and settled him in his basket in a warm spot by the cooker. He was still limp and shivering. Carole quickly heated some milk for him.

Moments later, Neil was crouching down beside Jake and offering him the bowl of warm milk. The puppy lapped feebly at it and then closed his eyes.

"He's ill," Neil said anxiously.

"He just needs to warm up," Carole said. "Come away. Let him rest for a bit."

Neil tried to carry on helping his parents with the kennel work but he was finally overcome with distraction.

Looking in on him for the umpteenth time, Neil was still worried. Jake wasn't properly asleep. He kept twitching and whimpering, and he didn't want his milk.

Neil dragged his father back into the kitchen for a second opinion. "I think we should take him to see Mike," Neil said.

Mike Turner took care of all the dogs in King Street Kennels. Neil knew that if there was anything seriously wrong with Jake he couldn't be in better hands.

"Mike might not be at the surgery," Bob said. "It's Christmas Eve. And it'll be difficult to get there in this."

"It's stopped snowing," Carole said, overhearing their conversation as she stepped inside. "And the Preston's van hasn't turned up yet. If Mike is there, I could go to the Cash and Carry and take Jake on the same trip."

Bob nodded. It was probably best to make sure the pup hadn't caught anything serious.

Carole went out into the hall to telephone the vet.

Neil crouched anxiously over Jake, stroking his silky head. Sam came close and nosed his son, almost as if he was worrying as well.

"Mike's at the surgery," Carole said as she came back into the room. "He'll see Jake if we go right away. He was just about to leave for the holidays – I only just caught him. Emily, you'd better come with me and hold Jake on your lap."

Neil stood up. "Why can't I go? Jake's my dog."

"Because you'll be more help here," Carole said.

"Your mother's right," Bob added, before Neil could protest again. "I need you here. If the Preston's van turns up, you'll have to help me carry boxes. There's still paths to clear, and the runs, and—"

"But I've shovelled snow all morning," Neil muttered rebelliously. "It's not fair."

"Neil," Bob said, "we had enough trouble from you first thing this morning. Don't start being difficult now. Besides, which is more important, getting Jake to the vet quickly or standing here arguing?"

"I know . . ." It was hard for Neil to admit his dad was right. "You'd better look after him," he said to Emily, as she slipped into her winter coat.

"Of course I will," she said sympathetically, swathing Jake in a blanket from his basket so that only his nose poked out of the folds. "I promise, Neil."

When Carole and Emily had gone, Bob let Neil take the dogs one or two at a time into the barn for some play and exercise, while he cleaned out the pens. It was just the sort of job Neil liked, and at any other time he would have enjoyed himself. Now he was just worried about Jake, and wishing he could have gone with him instead of Emily. Sarah, however, was quite happy singing Christmas songs to the dogs.

"Time for a break," Bob said, as he collected the last two dogs from Kennel Block One. "No sign of the Preston's van yet."

As Neil followed his father from the barn, the snow was falling again and refused to give up its relentless deluge of King Street Kennels and the Compton area. Huge feathery flakes were already piling up over ground they had cleared that morning. The Range Rover's tracks from just a couple of hours before were already invisible. Sarah, clasping her dad's hand, was having trouble tripping her way through the deep blanket of snow.

"Mum's not back yet," Neil said.

Bob glanced at his watch. "She's been gone long enough." He frowned, and added thoughtfully, "Quite long enough to see Mike and then go on to the Cash and Carry. The snow must be holding her up."

"Or maybe there's something really bad

wrong with Jake!" Neil said, panicky all over again.

"I doubt it," Bob said, reassuring him. He pushed open the kitchen door and Neil followed him inside, shaking snow off himself. "If you're really worried," his dad went on, "I'll try giving Mike a ring."

With Neil at his heels, he went out to the telephone in the passage and dialled the surgery number. Neil could just hear the faint ringing; it went on and on, until the answering machine cut in. Starting to feel desperate, Neil said, "Where is he?"

"The message says they're closed now until Monday," Bob said, starting to dial another number. "Which suggests that your mum made it to the surgery. Mike wouldn't have left when he knew she was coming. I'll try him on his mobile."

He gave a nod to Neil as this time someone answered the call. "Hello . . . Mike?"

Neil could hear the speaker at the other end, but not the words he was saying. He shifted restlessly from foot to foot and tried to make sense of his dad's end of the conversation.

"They did . . . Great. And Jake? Yes . . . yes, I see. Fine." He stuck a thumb up and grinned at

Neil. Neil felt suddenly shaky with relief. "And they left when? Oh . . . no, she was going to the Cash and Carry, for dog food. Yes, I know . . . yes. It was?" Bob listened for a long time and then said, "OK, Mike, thanks. It's probably nothing to worry about. Cheerio . . . and Happy Christmas."

He put the phone down, frowning again.

"How's Jake?" Neil asked anxiously.

"Oh, Jake's fine. Mike says he was starting to perk up already by the time he got to the surgery. He was exhausted more than anything else. He just needs rest and warmth."

Neil felt a big grin spread over his face. "That's great!"

"Mike closed the surgery as soon as your mum left. He went home, and he tells me the snow ploughs had been out on the main Compton to Padsham road, so he didn't have much trouble getting there."

"Then where's Mum?" Neil asked. "Why hasn't she brought Jake home?"

"That's what I'd like to know," said Bob. "She's had plenty of time to get to the Cash and Carry. So where are they now?"

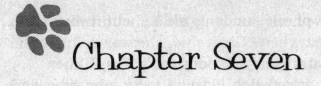

Chapter Seven

Neil and Bob stood in the passage staring at each other. Then Bob shook himself.

"I'm losing my mind," he said, slapping his forehead. "Your mum took the mobile phone with her. I can call her on that."

He picked up the phone again and dialled a number.

Neil bit his lip.

Bob started to shake his head. "Nope. 'Fraid I'm getting a number unobtainable message. The battery must have run out."

"So what do we do now?"

"Listen, Neil, I'm going to get on outside. There's nothing we *can* do stuck here. You stay near a phone, and give me a shout if your mum calls."

"And what if she doesn't?"

Bob frowned, and tugged at his beard. "We'll worry about that later. Come on, Sarah, are you going to help me out again?"

When his father and Sarah had gone outside, Neil went back to the kitchen. After all the worry about Jake, he realized that he was starving again. He pulled off his jacket and boots, poured himself some milk, and made a jam sandwich. Then he gave Sam a couple of dog biscuits. Sitting at the table, he ruffled the Border collie's fur.

"They'll be back soon, Sam," he said. "Everything'll be fine. You'll see."

Sam looked up at him, his eyes bright and trusting. Neil hoped that he was telling him the truth.

He hadn't been waiting in the kitchen long when Sarah skipped in, singing *Jingle Bells*. The trouble was, she only knew the first line. You could have too much of anything.

"Do you have to?" Neil said in mock exasperation.

Sarah gave him a black look. "Don't be so rude. Jingle bells, jingle bells, jingle all—" She broke off as if a thought had struck her. "Neil, will Father Christmas be able to get here, through all this snow?"

Neil sighed. "He drives a sledge."

Sarah thought about this for a moment, and a beaming smile spread over her face. "That's all right, then. Cos I wrote to him and asked him to bring Denny back for Beth and Gina."

"He might not be able—"

"Yes, he will! Father Christmas is magic. He can do anything. Jingle bells, jingle bells . . ."

To Neil's relief, his little sister skipped off again, back outside to help Bob. Probably driving him mad with *Jingle Bells*, Neil thought. All the same, he wished she wasn't so confident. Her Christmas would be spoilt if Denny still wasn't found.

Sarah's footsteps had hardly died away when the phone rang. Neil shot out into the passage.

"King Street Kennels."

At first all he could hear was crackling. He raised his voice. "Hello . . . hello? I can't hear you."

Then words started to come through.

"Neil, it's Mum—"

Through the interference Neil could hardly recognize her voice.

"Listen, we're—"

"What was that?"

". . . battery's running out. We're—"

Neil gritted his teeth in frustration as the voice was drowned out in another wash of crackling. When it came back his mum was saying, ". . . over the bridge and up the hill. Have you got that, Neil?"

"No!" Neil was starting to panic. "I didn't hear the first bit. Where are you?"

Carole's voice came again, obviously

73

shouting, but sounding hardly any louder. "Can't get back . . . Emily's hurt, she—" More crackling. ". . . to help Jake."

"Jake?" Neil repeated, more alarmed than ever. "What about Jake? What's wrong?"

This time nothing but the crackling noise replied. The connection went dead.

He put down the phone and then tried ringing his mother's mobile phone number.

It was still unobtainable.

Giving up at last, he went outside to find his father.

Bob had no more success than Neil at getting through to the mobile phone.

"She said Emily was hurt!" Neil kept repeating. "And something's the matter with Jake. She said something about helping Jake!"

He couldn't stop trying to make sense of the few scraps of news that had come through. "What are we going to do?"

Bob took a deep breath. "I'm going to ring the police."

"But we don't even know where Mum is!"

"They can put out a call to all cars to look out for her. That's more than we can do, stuck here without transport." He started to dial again.

"Take it easy, Neil. Panicking won't help. In this sort of weather, a few cars are bound to get stuck here and there."

Neil couldn't bear to go on listening. He went back into the kitchen. The few words of his mum's phone call kept churning around in his mind. If only the battery hadn't failed! There was a spare in the office. She should have taken it with her.

Then Neil started to think. If his mum was stuck, if Emily was hurt and something – Neil didn't let himself wonder what – had happened to Jake, she might not be able to leave them to get to a proper phone. What could he do to help her? If someone took them the spare battery, then Carole could call the police, or an ambulance, or a breakdown service for the car, or whatever she wanted. But there wasn't anyone to do it. Except me, Neil thought. And I don't know where she is.

He considered the garbled phone call again. His mum had said, ". . . over the bridge and up the hill."

The Cash and Carry was over the other side of Compton, across the river and about as far as it could be from King Street Kennels. The route Carole would have taken was well used, and if she was stuck there she could easily have found someone to give them a lift or take a message. But she hadn't, so they were somewhere else. Carole must have had a reason to turn off the main road. Neil's mind was racing with possibilities.

On this side of the river was a whole maze of minor roads and lanes, leading over the hills and dropping down again to rejoin the main road on the King Street side of town. What Neil's mum had said would fit if she was up there somewhere. Neil swallowed, and clenched his fists.

"I'm going to do it!" he said aloud.

Just then Bob came into the kitchen; Neil wondered if he'd heard, but all he said was, "Stay by the phone, Neil", and went outside.

Feeling like a thief, Neil crept down the passage to the office and slid the spare phone battery into his pocket. As he was putting his jacket and boots on again, Sam came padding up to him. His head was cocked and his tail waved hopefully. Neil stooped and patted him.

"Poor old boy, you've been stuck inside for ages. But you can't—"

He broke off, and poked his head outside the back door. Since he had been indoors the snow had stopped completely. A pale, watery sun had broken through the cloud, and the surface of the snow glittered faintly. Neil thought it wasn't as cold as it had been. He went back to Sam.

"OK, boy, why not?" he said. "It's not so bad out there now, and you could do with a walk." Sam needed his exercise like all the other dogs, after all. "Let's go and find Jake, shall we?"

Cautiously Neil emerged into the courtyard, with Sam following him on a lead. He couldn't see his dad, but he could hear barking from the rescue centre, and he guessed Bob was in there. Swiftly he led the Border collie across the courtyard and out through the side gate. He didn't relax, or stop listening for his father's voice behind him, until he was down the drive and out onto the Compton road.

To begin with, Neil turned away from Compton, along the road for a little way, and then climbed over a stile leading to a footpath. That would take him in an almost direct line to the area he wanted to search. Sam hopped deftly over the stile behind him, reminding Neil of how clever he had once been at Agility competitions. He stood beside Neil on the other side, tongue lolling, head up as if he was asking, "Which way now?"

The footpath itself was obscured by snow, but the outline of it, alongside a hedge, was easy to follow, and from time to time there were small yellow waymarks, intended for country walkers. Neil knew this terrain well, but it was almost unrecognizable under its thick coat of snow. He felt thankful for the friendly dog trotting along beside him.

The smooth layer of fresh, untrodden snow covered uneven places in the ground, so Neil kept stumbling into holes he could not see. Snow trickled down over the tops of his boots and slowly began to turn his feet to lumps of ice. Once he slipped and fell. As he got up painfully, brushing snow off himself, he realized that he might get hurt. If he was stuck up here alone, probably no one would find him. He hadn't even left a note. For a few seconds he stood still, shivering and looking back. Had he done the right thing? Then, swallowing his fear, he went on.

His determination renewed, the going became easier as the footpath joined a farm track, where there were wheel marks for Neil and Sam to walk in. Before it reached the farm itself, another footpath led off to a second stile and a lane. Its surface was unmarked; no cars had been along there recently, but at least it was more solid underfoot.

Neil felt a rising excitement. He was getting close now to the area where he might expect to find his mum, Emily and Jake. He led Sam along the lane, uphill, because they would need to cross the ridge of moorland that surrounded Compton on this side.

They had not gone far when Neil realized that the sun had gone. Grey clouds were massing overhead again, and flakes of snow began to drift down, growing heavier with every step Neil took. He glanced down at Sam, padding undaunted alongside him.

"Thanks for sticking with me, boy. Not long now," he muttered.

As the bushes and trees on either side of the road thinned out, Neil became more conscious of the wind. It swirled snow in front of him so his eyes started to hurt as he tried to see his way. It drove snow into his face. His skin stung with it and his bare cheeks glowed bright red. He couldn't feel his feet any longer, and his hands were starting to go numb. He wound Sam's lead around his wrist, in case he should accidentally let go of the loop.

After what seemed like hours, but was

probably less than fifteen minutes, Neil realized that the upward slope was levelling out. They must be up on the ridge. He swallowed a gulp of snowfilled air, and bent down to pat Sam.

Snow was matted in Sam's coat, but the Border collie didn't seem at all bothered. He gave Neil's hand a friendly lick, and padded on into the wind. Neil began to wonder if he had been right to bring him.

He was finding it harder to see his way. The road stretched across the moor, with nothing on each side but a ditch. A few paces further on he tripped over a cattle grid, and barely saved himself from falling again. He kept veering from side to side, and only realized it when he saw the ditch open in front of him. Once he startled two or three sheep, huddling together in the shelter of a rock; they broke and ran off, bleating.

"Sorr-ee!" Neil cried after them.

Neil was so tired he could barely keep moving, but he knew it would be fatal to stop. People who were lost in the snow could lie down and go to sleep, and never get up again.

"We're not lost, are we, Sam?" he said, to comfort himself as much as the dog. "We know where we are."

He was beginning to feel really frightened, not for himself, but for Sam. How could he have been so stupid, to bring a sick dog out in weather like this? He should have known the snow would start again. He even stopped and peered round through the curtain of snow, but he could see nothing through the whirling whiteness. There was no shelter, and it was too late to go back.

As he went on, Neil realized that instead of walking correctly at heel, Sam had taken the lead. Instead of trying to guide them both through the snow, Neil started to follow. Straight away, the going was easier. He just had to keep on putting one foot in front of the other, shield his eyes as best he could from the driving snow, and let Sam find their way.

Soon they started to go downwards again. They crossed another cattle grid, and gradually more bushes appeared beside the road, sheltering Neil and Sam from the worst of the wind. It was easier for Neil to see, and he started to feel more hopeful; now he really might stand a chance of finding his family.

Not long after, they came to a crossroads. There was no sign to give Neil any idea of which direction to take, and Sam seemed to want to go straight on. Neil was too tired by now to do

anything except let him have his way.

But about a hundred metres down the road, Neil had to stop. In front of him was a tumbled wall of snow, reaching above his head. Neil wasn't sure where it came from – blown there by the wind, or abandoned by a snow plough, or deposited like an avalanche from the hillside above. He only knew that there was no obvious way round it.

"Bad idea, Sam," he said.

Together he and the dog slogged back up the hill. Going over ground they had already covered made Neil feel even more exhausted.

When he reached the crossroads again, he stooped beside Sam. The Border collie stood with his head down. His breath was coming fast, and Neil could feel a rapid heartbeat. It was vital to find somewhere the dog could rest.

As he straightened up, Neil realized something else. Although the snow was slackening off, he could not see more than a few metres in any direction. Darkness was falling. The thought of how stupid he'd been hit Neil again. In the dark he wouldn't be able to find anything, not even his own way home.

"Left or right, Sam?" Neil asked. A lot depended on that decision. Sam just panted, obviously exhausted.

The left hand road looked as if it led up to the moor again. On the right the lane turned a sharp corner. Neil tugged on Sam's lead.

"OK, boy. Right it is."

This road twisted gradually downwards. Finally Neil came to a place where it seemed to zigzag back on itself and start leading back up.

"Oh, no," Neil groaned. Was he never going to get off the moor?

He kept trudging on, Sam padding wearily at his heels. Then as he came to the next bend, he halted. After rising a little way, the road dipped again.

And below him, at the bottom of the dip, barely visible in the dying light, was the King Street Kennels Range Rover.

"Mum!" Neil yelled. "Emily!"

Energy flooded through him again. Slipping and sliding, he dashed down the road. Seeming just as excited, Sam bounded after him. The slope was so steep that Neil was only able to stop when he crashed into the side of the car sending a wodge of snow sliding off the roof.

"Mum?" he said uncertainly.

The Range Rover was tipped forward, with its front wheels in a ditch at the side of the road. The windows were frosty on the outside and misted up inside. Neil dashed snow out of his eyes and scraped a circle of ice off one of the side windows. He tried to peer into the car, but he couldn't see anything.

"Mum!" he called, more loudly now.

He tried the driver's door, but it was locked. So was the rear door on the same side. Neil floundered through the snow around the back of the Range Rover. The ground gave way under him as he slid into the ditch. In his fall, he grabbed the handle of the rear door on the other side, and it swung open.

Apart from some crates of dog food, the Range Rover was completely empty. Carole and Emily and Jake were gone.

Chapter Eight

For a minute Neil stood and stared at the Range Rover. He couldn't think what to do. His plan didn't cover this.

He tried to work out where his mum, Emily and Jake might be. Perhaps they'd left the car and tried to walk home, and that was how Emily had been hurt. But his mum surely had more sense than to try doing that in heavy snow, especially when they had a small puppy to carry.

More likely, Neil thought, they'd been picked up, by the police or by a passing driver. Maybe they were safe at home now, while he was stuck here. Neil groaned aloud. His mum and dad would be furious with him when he got back!

But even that would be better than spending the night out here, and not getting home at all.

Neil used the car door to heave himself out of the ditch. Looking around in the gathering darkness he saw a spot of something bright on the snow further down the lane. "Stay, Sam," he said.

Leaving the Border collie to rest by the car, Neil struggled down the lane until he reached the bright object. When he picked it up, brushing snow off it, he saw it was Emily's crimson scarf. There were marks in the snow, too, though Neil could not make out what they were.

Just beside him was a five-barred gate; the snow was pushed away on the other side, as if someone had opened it recently. There were more marks on the hillside beyond, though the snow and the wind had partly erased them.

"Sam!" he called. "Sam!"

The Border collie came trotting towards him; Neil pointed up the hill. "Let's take a look, boy."

Sam squeezed through the space between the gate and the hedge, and scrambled away, scattering snow as he went. Neil clambered over the gate and struggled upwards in his wake, floundering in deep, loose drifts.

"Sam, wait for me!" he shouted.

Suddenly Sam was there again, pawing eagerly at his knees. Neil grabbed the lead. "You daft dog. What have you found?"

Sam let out a single bark, as if he was answering. Looking upwards, Neil could make out the shape of a building, black against the darkening sky. Hope surged through him, and died as he realized it wasn't a house, just a barn or a shed with blank walls.

"Sam, that's not—"

Neil's voice was cut off as Sam's bark sounded again, and as if in reply a light appeared ahead of them, by the dark building. Not light from a window; it looked more like a torch.

Neil took a few more paces, toiling up the hillside, feet slipping under him. Then he was flooded with relief as he started to make out the figure holding the torch, and heard a voice calling, "Neil? Is that you?"

It was Neil's mum.

The barn was stacked with bales of hay. Carole had pulled some of them out to make a cosy nest where Emily sat with one leg stretched out in front of her. Jake was curled up asleep in a blanket on her lap. But what made Neil stand gaping, when Carole guided him into shelter, was the other dog, lying nose on forepaws, by Emily's side. It was Denny.

"You've found him!" he exclaimed. "Is he OK?"

"Fine," said Emily. "He's lost his collar somehow, but he's not hurt."

"But what happened? What are you doing here?"

"I could ask you that," Carole said. "Coming out in weather like this by yourself was really stupid. And bringing Sam. What if you'd got lost?"

Neil wasn't going to tell her how close he had come, up on the moor. In fact, he felt so exhausted that he wasn't sure he could tell the story at all.

Carole must have seen how tired he was, because she stopped asking questions, just pushed him further into the barn and closed the door tightly against the harsh weather outside.

"OK," she said. "Our story first. But you'd better have a really good explanation when it's your turn."

She switched off the torch to save the battery and settled down in the hay beside Emily. Now the barn was dimly lit from windows high up under the roof. Neil collapsed on the floor on the other side of Denny. After so long out in the snow, the barn felt warm; he stripped off his gloves and pushed back the hood of his jacket.

To Neil's relief, Sam seemed none the worse for his struggle through the snow. He shook himself, scattering snow everywhere, and flopped down panting, his tongue hanging out in a satisfied grin. Neil grinned tiredly back.

"Go on, Mum," he said. "What happened?"

Carole began by telling Neil about the visit to Mike Turner, and how Mike had reassured them that Jake would be fine.

"Then we went to the Cash and Carry. That was fine, too. We bought what we needed and set off home. And that's where our problems started.

"There must have been some sort of accident or hold-up on the main road, because there was a queue of cars stretching right back to the bridge. We were about half an hour just inching along. So when we came to the turn-off on to the moor, I decided to be clever and drive home by the back roads."

She swiped a hand across her forehead, pushing away straggling dark hair.

"It was fine to start with. But the snow on the road was really thick, and even the Range Rover started to skid."

"And we ended up in the ditch," said Emily.

"So why didn't you stay with the car?" Neil asked. "I was scared stiff when I found it and you weren't there."

"You can thank Jake for that," Carole went on. "Emily and I got out to see if we could push the car out of the ditch. Not a hope, of course. We left Jake in the back, and then before we

90

knew what had happened, he'd taken off down the lane."

"I ran after him," Emily explained. "And I fell and sprained my ankle." She tried to move the outstretched leg, and winced.

"We'll hope it's just a sprain," Carole said. "Anyway, I chased after Jake, and I caught him just outside here. He was yapping fit to bust. And just before I started to carry him back to the car, I heard another dog barking inside. I had a look, and it was Denny!"

"Jake found him!" A beaming smile spread over Neil's face. "He's a real tracker dog!" He stared at the sleeping puppy. "I don't believe it!"

He guessed that Jake had just been feeling mischievous, but if his yapping had made Denny reply, that was good enough for Neil.

"So I helped Emily up here. I thought it would be warmer than the car," Carole went on. "That's when I tried to phone, but the battery was too low. I could kick myself for not bringing the spare with me."

Neil felt a sudden warm flood of triumph. He had almost forgotten about the mobile phone battery in all the confusion of the journey, but now he pulled it out of the pocket of his jeans.

"You mean this?" he asked innocently.

Carole stared at it. "Neil . . . you didn't? That's unbelievable! I thought we were stuck here all night, for sure."

She slid the mobile phone out of the inside pocket of her jacket, and fitted the spare battery. "Neil," she said as she punched in their home number, "I think you've just got yourself out of trouble."

Neil grinned. A few seconds later he heard a voice at the other end, as the phone was answered.

"Bob?" his mum said. "Yes, it's me. We're stuck in a barn somewhere. Neil found us and – oh." She flashed a look at Neil, and handed him the phone.

"Neil, I've been frantic!" Bob's voice came through clearly. "You shouldn't have gone off like that without asking."

"But you wouldn't have let me go," Neil protested. "And Mum and Emily would—"

"I've got the police out looking for you as well now!" his dad interrupted.

"Well . . ." Neil started to feel guilty. "I guess I could have left a note. But I'm fine, honestly, Dad. And you should have seen Sam! He—"

"Neil, put your mother on again. But don't think you've heard the last of this. We'll have a talk when you get home. A very serious one."

"OK, Dad. Bye."

Neil handed the phone back to his mum.

He was glad that he wasn't going home straight away. His dad probably needed some time to cool down – but Neil wasn't too worried about getting a stern dressing-down. He was confident he had done the right thing in setting out on his marathon journey with Sam.

Carole finished telling Bob what had happened, and then called the police to ask for help. Not really listening, Neil leant over to stroke the sleeping Jake.

"Beth and Gina will be over the moon," he said to Emily. "Do you think the pantomime will go on now?"

"Yes, I suppose . . ." Emily broke off, and her eyes filled with tears. "But I'll be out of it now, with this stupid ankle!"

"That's tough," said Neil. "I'm really sorry. Still," he added, "Denny's safe, and that's the main thing."

Emily sniffed, and nodded. "Yes, I know. But Neil, there's something else—"

She was interrupted again as Carole put the phone back into her pocket and said, "The police are on their way. We'll be out of here before we know it."

"I hope so," Emily said. "That's what we haven't told you, Neil. When Mum found Denny in here the door was shut. There was no way he could have got in by himself."

"You mean someone shut him in here?" Neil asked.

Carole nodded. "I don't know why, but it looks as if somebody is keeping him here. And whoever he is, I really hope the police arrive before he gets back."

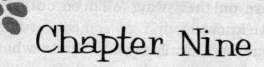

Chapter Nine

By now the barn was almost dark. Neil could barely make out the shapes of Emily and his mum or the dogs. Everything was quiet except for little scuttling noises in the hay, and an occasional snuffling from Jake in his sleep.

"Neil," Carole said, "do you think you could go down to the car and wait there for the police? They shouldn't be long, and I don't want to miss them."

"Er, sure," Neil said, groping to find the gloves he had taken off.

Before he could get up they all heard footsteps scrunch in the snow outside the barn, and someone whistling a tune. Then both footsteps and whistling stopped, and were followed by the sound of someone fumbling with the door catch. Emily audibly drew breath. Neil felt his heart start to pound. He got to his feet, and his mum switched on the torch as the door swung open.

A man stood in the entrance, shielding his eyes from the light. He was tall, wearing a long ragged overcoat tied round his waist with hairy string. Even though there was snow on the ground he wore scruffy trainers, which gaped at the toes. He carried a bulging plastic carrier bag.

Carole lowered the torch slightly and the man took his hand away from his eyes to reveal sharp features pinched with cold, surrounded by a bush of straggly white hair and beard. He was peering suspiciously at the Parkers.

"Who are you?" he asked. "What're you doing here?"

To Neil's surprise, it was Emily who replied. "Did you steal Denny?" she demanded fiercely. "The Wards aren't cruel to him. They're not!"

She tried to struggle upright and face him. Disturbed, Jake shot off her lap, yapping frantically, and hurled himself at the newcomer's trainers. Sam got to his feet, a low growling deep in his throat. Alarmed, the old man took a step back.

Only Denny stayed calm. He got up and trotted over to the man, who stooped and petted him, a smile spreading over his face.

"There's a good lad," he said. "Want to see what I've got for you?"

Neil started to realize that this wasn't an Animal Rights protester, even one crazy enough to steal a dog to make his point. And anyone

who was that fond of a dog couldn't be all bad. Neil told Sam to sit, and scooped up Jake before he could make any more holes in the man's trainers.

"Emily, calm down." Carole had relaxed, as if she too realized that the newcomer was not a threat. "This dog belongs to some friends of ours," she told him. "They've been really worried."

"I didn't steal him, missus," the old man said. "I found him wandering. He weren't wearing a collar. I'd have taken him home if I'd known where he lived." He bent down again and scratched Denny's ears. "Denny's your name, eh? I called him Snowy," he explained, "cos it was snowing when I found him."

"He had a collar when he went missing." Emily was still suspicious. "And you could have taken him to the police."

"There weren't no hurry," the man said defensively. "Me and him, we found somewhere warm to stay, didn't we, lad? And then I went off to get us both something to eat."

He came further into the barn and started to rummage around in his carrier bag. From it he produced a rather soggy parcel and spread out the wrappings in front of Denny.

"There we are, lad. Nice bit o' liver."

Denny started to eat hungrily. Sam showed no interest, but Jake wriggled in Neil's arms, yipping in a frenzy, and the old man, his wrinkled face creased into a smile, gave him a scrap of the liver in his fingers.

"He's a fine little fellow," he said. "Is he yours, son?"

"Yes, his name's Jake. I'm Neil Parker, and this is my mum, Carole, and my sister Emily."

The old man ducked his head.

"Pleased to meet you, missus. They just call me Nick. I didn't mean no harm, you know," he said to Emily.

Emily smiled, but Neil thought she still didn't look entirely sure that she wanted to trust Nick. Neil suspected that the old man was lonely, and might have been putting off the time when he would have to give Denny up. At least he'd kept him safe, when he might have died of cold.

"You can come with us when we take him home," he said. "The Wards will want to thank you, and—"

He was interrupted by the sound of a car engine labouring through the snow on the road at the foot of the hill. Blue light flashed on and off in the darkness outside the barn door.

"The police," said Carole.

Nick looked terrified.

"It's OK," Neil said. "We didn't call them because of Denny. Just to shift our car out of the ditch."

"I'll go down." Carole handed the torch to Neil. "You stay here where it's warm, and keep the dogs out of the way."

When she had gone, Nick started to unload more bits and pieces from his carrier bag, as if he was going to settle in.

"You're not staying here, are you?" Neil asked. "Haven't you got anywhere to live?"

Nick shook his head. "I've been on the road for years. Reckon I wouldn't feel right no more with a roof over my head."

"But tomorrow's Christmas!" Emily protested.

Nick shrugged.

"You can't spend Christmas in a barn!"

Neil hid a quiet grin. The best way for Emily to stop being suspicious of Nick was for her to find out that he was in trouble. Emily couldn't resist helping – dogs, people, you name it.

"Why don't you come to stay with us for Christmas?" she continued. "Mum and Dad wouldn't mind, would they, Neil?"

Neil wasn't sure about that, but still . . . it was Christmas. "No, of course they wouldn't."

Nick frowned and shook his head. "Don't reckon I could do that. Wouldn't be right."

Another car engine roared into life. The Range Rover! Neil looked out of the door and saw the police van, its blue light whirling, and the Range Rover with its lights on. A policeman in a bright yellow jacket was moving between the two vehicles.

"They've fixed a tow rope," Neil reported to Emily, who was trying to persuade Nick to change his mind. "The Range Rover's not moving though. I wonder if—"

He broke off as the police van slowly moved backwards, and the Range Rover lurched and almost leapt backwards out of the ditch.

"Yes!" Neil said. "They've done it!"

He went on watching as very slowly and carefully his mum turned the Range Rover so that it faced towards the main road again. Then she got out and climbed the hill to the barn, closely followed by the policeman.

". . . so if you could help me get her into the car, I'll take her straight to our doctor," Neil heard her say as she came into earshot.

"No problem," the policeman said, clapping

his hands together. He was a huge young man with a friendly grin. "Good heavens, you've got a right collection here, haven't you?" The grin faded as his eyes fell on Nick. "Who's this, then? He's not with you, is he?"

"Yes, he is!" Emily said, flying to Nick's defence.

"I'm not doing no harm," Nick said. "Just sheltering from the snow."

"Well, you can't shelter here, mate," the policeman said. "This is private property. You'll have to move on."

"In this?" Carole said. "Oh, come on, officer. You're not going to throw somebody out into the snow on Christmas Eve?"

The young policeman looked uncomfortable. "I'm sorry, ma'am, but the law's the law. There's a fire hazard, for one thing, if he stays here. Come on, mate. Let's go."

Muttering under his breath, Nick had already started to pack up his belongings into the plastic bag.

"Mum," Neil said, "this is horrible. Can't he come and stay with us for Christmas?"

"Please, Mum!" Emily added.

"Well . . ."

Carole was starting to smile, but the

policeman interrupted her. "It's not a good idea, ma'am, if I may say so."

"No you may not," Carole said crisply. "Who I invite into my house is my affair. This gentleman has already been very helpful in looking after our friends' dog, and if he wants to come to stay with us he's very welcome. Please come and spend Christmas with us, Nick."

Nick still looked doubtful, glancing from Carole to the policeman and back again. Inspired, Neil said, "We run King Street Kennels. We've got lots of dogs for you to meet."

"You could give us a hand with them if you like," said Carole.

Nick's face lit up, and creased again into a pleased smile. "Well, missus, if you're sure . . ."

"That's settled then," said Carole. "Now, officer, if you could just give Emily a hand, we can all get moving."

Everyone slowly made their way down the hill towards the waiting cars. Carole went first, followed by the policeman carrying Emily. Nick came next with Sam and Denny padding after him. Last of all, closing the barn door carefully behind him, came Neil with Jake bundled inside his jacket. He wasn't going to risk the little dog running off again.

The policeman helped Emily into the back of the Range Rover, and went back to his own van where another policeman was waiting.

"I was going to take you to Casualty," Carole explained to Emily. "But the policeman tells me they've got queues a mile long. So I rang Dr Harvey, and he says that if we go round there he'll see us at home. He's already closed for the holidays." Briskly she added, "Neil, can you get the dogs into the back? Nick, you sit next to me."

When he was in the back of the car, surrounded by dogs, Neil leant over and murmured into Emily's ear, "Don't you there's something funny about this? Nick – Nicholas – bushy white beard . . . ?"

Emily started to giggle, but the engine starting up covered the sound.

"Better hope Squirt doesn't catch on," Neil added. "She always said Father Christmas would bring Denny back!"

Chapter Ten

Dr Harvey gently examined Emily's ankle.

"You've got a nasty sprain there," he said. "But that's all it is. I'm sure it's not broken. I'll put a bandage on it, and you've got to stay off the foot as much as you can for the next few days."

"Thank goodness it's no worse," said Carole.

The Parkers were huddled round the fire in Alex Harvey's sitting room. Finn and Sandy, the doctor's two dogs, lay on the hearthrug and watched his every move. Finn was a Kerry blue, a real show dog, while Sandy was just an ordinary mutt, but now that the two of them had settled down together they were the best of friends, and Alex loved them both.

Carole had left Sam and Denny in the car with Nick to look after them, but Neil had insisted on bringing Jake inside. The tiny Border collie scrambled around on his lap, eager to get down and make friends, but Neil kept him firmly out of the way. Finn at least could be a bit uncertain in temper at times. Besides, Neil didn't dare think what Jake might do with a bandage!

"You've got a lively one there," Dr Harvey said as he fastened Emily's bandage in place. He leant over and tickled Jake. "Are we going to see him winning all the Agility prizes like his dad?"

"Maybe," Neil said.

"No, he's a tracker dog," Emily contradicted.

Dr Harvey laughed. "Is he really? Isn't he a bit small for a bloodhound?"

"You could try training him for obedience *and* tracking events," Carole said. "But there's time enough to think about that when he's bigger. Let's get Christmas over first." She got up and started to put her coat back on. "Are you going away for Christmas, Alex?"

Dr Harvey looked gloomy.

"I was going over to my sister and her family in York. But all the roads across the Pennines are closed because of the snow. I'll never get there now."

"That's awful!" said Emily. She exchanged a look with her mother and Neil. "Mum, couldn't we . . ."

"Yes, of course we could. Alex, you're coming to have Christmas dinner with us. And Finn and Sandy, of course."

The doctor's face broke into a smile. "If you're sure . . ."

"No problem. Bob bought a turkey big enough to feed half of Compton. You're very welcome, Alex."

"Then in that case . . ." Alex Harvey's grin broadened, "we'd be delighted. All three of us."

"Ace!" said Neil.

"Come about twelve noon," Carole said as the doctor carried Emily out to the car. "Things should be livening up about then."

Neil looked up at the sky. The snow had almost stopped, though a few stray flakes were still drifting down.

"I hope you don't get stuck," he said.

"Don't worry," Dr Harvey promised. "I'll get there. Even if I have to borrow a sledge and harness Finn and Sandy!"

*

Back in the car, Carole turned for home.

"We'll drop Denny off on the way," she said. "It's a good thing it's not far."

The lights were on in the Wards' house when the Range Rover pulled up outside. Neil hurried up the path and rang the bell. Emily refused to stay in the car and hobbled after Nick and Carole who had brought Denny.

Beth Ward opened the door and stood frozen, staring at Denny at Nick's feet.

"Oh it is!" she said at last. "Oh, thank you! You've really found him."

"Beth?" It was Gina's voice. "Who are you—"

She came up the passage behind Beth, and broke off as she saw Denny. The retriever bounded away from Nick, barking eagerly and licking Gina's face as she hugged him.

"Easy to see he's yours," Nick said, a bit sadly.

"But where did you find him?" Beth asked. "His collar's gone – and Emily, what happened to you? Oh, come in, everybody, and tell us all about it."

They all crowded into the Wards' tiny kitchen. Gina went to fetch her mother to hear the good news, while Beth found a chair for Emily. Neil let Jake and Sam roam around

while he and Emily told the story, with additions now and again from their mother and Nick.

"So it's you we've really got to thank," Mrs Ward said to Nick, when they had finished. "I'm sure Denny would have died of cold if you hadn't looked after him. You naughty boy!" she added to Denny. "Don't you dare wander off like that again!"

Denny, with his face in a bowl of food, didn't

seem too bothered by the scolding. Mrs Ward took out her purse and emptied it of notes, which she held out to Nick.

"Don't be offended," she said. "But I'm sure you can make good use of this. And Denny's worth ten times as much to us."

Nick grinned. "I don't offend easy, missus." He took the notes and stowed them away inside his ragged overcoat. "Thanks. It were a pleasure to look after him. He's a grand dog."

"He's really clever!" Emily said. "Beth, show Nick some of Denny's tricks."

Denny had finished feeding, so Beth snapped her fingers to get his attention, shook hands with him, and made him beg for a biscuit and jump over her outstretched arm.

"It's silly to think he doesn't enjoy it," Emily said.

"I wouldn't force him," Beth said, petting Denny and rewarding him with a biscuit. "All right, trouble, here you are," she added to Jake, who trotted up to her and pushed his nose into her hand. She gave him a biscuit, and one to Sam, who had better manners, but was looking on hopefully. "At least now we can forget about that horrid phone call. It wasn't anything to do with Animal Rights at all."

"Glen told us none of his friends would steal a dog," said Emily.

"So all we have to worry about now is the pantomime," said Gina.

"Will it still go on?" Neil asked.

"Yes, of course it will!" Beth sounded cheerful and determined. "We've still got a week. Now that Denny's back we can do anything! Emily, I'll give you a ring about rehearsals on Boxing Day, OK?"

"But I've hurt my ankle," Emily said. Neil could see she was trying hard not to cry. "I can't be in it."

"Oh, yes, you can," said Beth. "I'm not having you drop out now; not when you've done so much to get Denny back."

"Dr Harvey says I mustn't walk on it."

"Then you can do your part sitting down." Beth refused to be put off. "Don't worry, I'll work it out. You can still sing, can't you?"

Emily started to smile, even though she had to wipe away a tear or two. Neil and the others pretended not to notice.

"And another thing, Neil," Beth went on. "I've been thinking. When we do the pantomime there are a lot of scenes where Denny isn't on. I've too much to do to look after him myself, and so has Gina, so I need somebody to be responsible for him. How would you like to be the pantomime's official dog handler?"

Neil stared at her. He'd resigned himself to being out of the pantomime altogether. Now he felt so pleased he thought he was going to burst.

"Dog handler?" he echoed. "You bet! That's what I do best!"

On the way home the roads were dark and silent. Very few cars were out. Carole drove slowly and carefully; the snow gleamed an eerie white in the car headlights. At long last the Range Rover turned into the drive of King Street Kennels.

"Made it!" said Carole.

As she switched off the engine the front door opened and Bob came down the steps.

"Are you all right?" he asked. "What took so long?"

Carole passed a hand over her face. Neil thought that she looked tired.

"It's a long story," she said. "I'll tell you in a few minutes. Can you take Emily indoors, while we put this dog food away?"

"Sure." Bob swung Emily up into his arms

and carried her off up the steps into the house. Neil thought he hadn't even noticed Nick.

Everyone else got out of the car. Neil had to give Sam a shove from behind; the Border collie had fallen asleep during the drive, but Neil thought he was none the worse for his excursion. He followed Neil through the side gate, while Carole and Nick unloaded the cases of dog food Carole had bought at the Cash and Carry.

Neil went to open up the store for his mother and Nick to begin stacking boxes, but the room already looked full.

"The Preston's van must have been," Carole said, pushing a strand of hair out of her eyes. "Wouldn't you just know! I needn't have gone to the Cash and Carry at all."

"And then we wouldn't have found Denny," Neil pointed out. "Or Nick."

From his cosy nest in Neil's jacket, Jake gave a little yap of agreement.

"All right, mutt," Neil said affectionately. "We all know you found him really."

It didn't take long for the extra food to be stored and Carole to close up the store room. Nick said to her:

"I see you've got a barn, missus."

"That's right."

"Mebbe I could sleep there, instead of in the house? I don't feel right under a roof. I've not slept in a proper bed for years."

"Well . . ."

Carole was hesitating, but Neil thought Nick's idea was a really good one. The barn was partially heated, and there was plenty of straw there, kept for the dogs' bedding. Nick could have blankets and a sleeping bag from the house. Now that he thought about it, Neil wouldn't have minded spending the night there himself.

"Emily'd be pleased," he said. "She won't have to share with Squirt."

"Well, Nick, if it's really what you'd prefer . . ." Carole said.

Nick's creased smile reappeared. "That'd be just grand, missus."

As they crossed the courtyard to the back door, Bob appeared. He bent down, stroked Sam's head, and felt for his heartbeat.

"Seems OK," he said, "but it wasn't a good idea to take him out like that, Neil. We'll keep an eye on him for a day or two, and if there seems to be a problem we'll call Mike."

He let Sam go, and the Border collie slipped past him into the house. Bob shook hands with Nick.

"Hello. Emily told me you looked after Denny. Welcome to King Street. I hear you're spending Christmas with us?"

"Seems like it, mister." Nick touched his forehead as if he might have lifted his cap to Bob. "And your missus says I might help with the dogs, like. I love dogs."

"That's fine, Nick. I'm sure we can find you some odd jobs to do."

While Nick and Bob were talking, Carole was tapping her foot impatiently. "Bob," she said, "do you think we could all go inside and get warm?"

"Yes – yes, of course." For the first time Neil thought his father was looking a bit agitated. Surely nothing else could go wrong now? "You see the Preston's delivery came?" his dad asked, still standing in the doorway. "Not long ago. I'd just about given them up."

"Yes, Bob," Carole said, starting to sound irritated. "But do we have to talk about it out here?"

"And there was an e-mail." Now Neil was sure his dad was talking for the sake of talking.

What was there inside the house that he didn't want Carole to see? "An e-mail from John Cartwright," Bob went on wildly. "He wishes us a Happy Christmas, and he says he's enjoying the sun, but it really isn't the same without Bernie. Next year he says he's going to be spending Christmas with his best friend."

Neil had to think about that, even while he wondered about his dad's strange behaviour. He'd imagined how pleased John Cartwright would be if he had managed to make Bernie into a proper rescue dog. But he'd failed so far. And now he realized that Bernie was already far more special than just another rescue dog. He was John Cartwright's best friend. Bernie didn't *need* any extra training.

"Bob," said Carole, with exaggerated patience, "why are we standing on the back step in the freezing cold talking about John Cartwright's e-mail?"

Bob looked sheepish. "There's something I should tell you—"

He grabbed at Carole's arm as she headed past him, missed, and made a face at Neil as they all trooped into the kitchen with Carole in the lead. Neil almost cannoned into his mum as she halted in the doorway.

"Bob!" she said. "What have you done?"

Peering round his mum, Neil stared into the kitchen. It was warm and bright. Delicious cooking smells were wafting from huge pots on top of the stove. At the kitchen table Emily was seated, with her injured foot on a stool. Sarah was sitting on the floor beside Sam's basket. Both had beaming smiles on their faces. But none of that was what made Neil stare.

The kitchen was full of dogs. Sam was in his basket. Two tiny white puppies, younger even than Jake, were scrambling all over Sarah and licking her face. A bull terrier with a white clown's face peered round the side of the old basket chair by the window. An Afghan hound, elegant and long-haired, was sprawled over most of the free floor space, while a black Scottie sat beside Emily, stumpy tail wagging as she scratched his wiry coat.

Carole blinked. "Bob – tell me I'm dreaming."

"Sorry," said Bob.

"These are the rescue dogs. What are they all doing in here?"

"That's what I was trying to tell you. The heating has gone off in the rescue centre, and I don't know what the matter is. And I won't be

able to get an engineer out until after Christmas." He spread his arms. "I had to put them somewhere."

But Bob . . ." Carole still looked appalled. "Bob, I've invited Alex Harvey for Christmas lunch. He'll bring Finn and Sandy as well."

"More dogs!" Sarah was delighted. "Lots of dogs for Christmas!"

Suddenly Carole's laughter bubbled up. She stood there shaking with it.

"If this is a dog's life," she gasped out when she could speak again, "then I can't get enough of it!"

Bob gave her a hug and went to start serving out the supper. Neil picked his way around assorted dogs to put Jake down beside Sam and fetch some food and water. He was turning back with the full bowls when he saw that Jake had grabbed Bob's slipper and was shaking it fiercely, growling and gnawing with tiny teeth.

"That's right, Jake," Neil said. "Save us from Dad's killer stinky slipper!"

He grinned across the kitchen at Emily, who grinned back.

"This is going to be a great Christmas," she said.

"A great Christmas," Neil agreed. "A real, doggy, Puppy Patrol Christmas!"

The Snow Dog

Chapter One

Neil Parker stamped his feet to keep them warm and pulled his cap further down over his spiky brown hair. The fresh wintry air felt biting cold after the warm train carriage he had left a few minutes ago.

"What's keeping Penny?" he asked. "She said she'd be here to meet us."

He was standing with his sister Emily on the station forecourt at Beckthwaite in the Lake District. Jake, his young black and white Border collie, barked and danced around, winding his lead around Neil's legs. He was a healthy and active dog, not much more than a puppy, with glossy fur and bright eyes.

"Give over, you daft dog," said Neil, laughing.

Jake looked up at him, his jaws wide open as if he was laughing too.

"Wow, it's cold!" said Emily, beginning to shiver. "Much colder than at home."

Eleven-year-old Neil and his younger sister Emily lived in the small country town of Compton, where their parents ran King Street Kennels, a boarding kennels and rescue centre. The Parkers were so keen on dogs that their friends called them the Puppy Patrol.

Back in Compton there wasn't any snow, but here it lay thick on the station roof, and long icicles hung from the gutters. Behind the station the hills were huge white mounds against a grey sky.

"I hope Penny likes the Christmas present I bought her," said Emily. "It's a book about—"

"There she is!" Neil interrupted, pointing at a large Range Rover which was turning into the station forecourt. As the car drew up beside Neil and Emily, Penny Ainsworth scrambled out of the back seat with her magnificent Great Dane, King. Her face was pink with cold but she was smiling broadly.

"Hi, Penny," said Neil. "How's King these days?" He ruffled the big dog's fur.

Neil and Emily had first met Penny when

they spent a week camping near Beckthwaite. King had been suffering from a serious eye condition which threatened his sight. It was mainly due to Neil that King had been able to have the operation he badly needed.

"King's fine," said Penny. "See for yourself!"

King was a huge dog with a honey-coloured coat, deep chest and strong legs. Neil bent over, took King's head in both hands, and peered at him. King accepted the examination calmly, looking back at Neil with eyes that were clear and undamaged.

"You're looking really well, aren't you, boy?" Neil held out one of the dog treats he always carried in his pocket. As King lowered his head to take it, Jake pushed his nose in, demanding his share of the titbits.

"This must be Jake," Penny said, ruffling the fur under his chin. "I've been looking forward to meeting him." Suddenly serious, she added, "Neil, I was sorry to hear about Sam."

Neil straightened up. "Yeah, well . . . "

He still found it hard to talk about Sam, Jake's dad and Neil's best friend. The Border collie had died heroically a few months before and Neil hadn't stopped missing him. This would be Neil's first Christmas without Sam and he wasn't looking forward to it.

"How's the film going?" Emily asked. Neil guessed she was tactfully trying to change the subject.

Penny's face lit up with enthusiasm. "It's very exciting! Max and Prince are great."

The film was why Neil and Emily were visiting Ainsworth Castle so close to Christmas. Their friend Max Hooper and his dog Prince were the stars of their favourite TV programme, *The Time Travellers*. On their previous visit he had been looking for a castle to use as Camelot in a

126

feature film about King Arthur. Ainsworth Castle was perfect. Although Penny's dad, Lord Ainsworth, had taken some persuading before he would allow the company to film there, he eventually saw the sense in it. The fee had paid for King's operation and helped with the Ainsworths' other money problems.

While they were talking, Lord Ainsworth had got out of the car. He was a tall man with a bristling moustache and a shapeless tweed hat rammed down over his ears.

He held out a hand to shake. "Neil and Emily. Welcome back."

"Thank you," said Emily. She always felt as if Penny's dad expected her to call him *sir*.

Lord Ainsworth heaved the Parkers' luggage into the car boot. "All aboard!" he said cheerfully.

"Do you mind if we walk?" Neil asked. "Jake hasn't had any exercise yet today, and he's been stuck on the train for ages."

"Whatever you like," said Lord Ainsworth.

He drove off, leaving Neil and the others to walk along the road which led from the station through the centre of the village. All the shops were bright with Yuletide decorations, and nearly every house had a Christmas tree in the window. The faint sound of Christmas carols drifted out from one of the shops and gave them all a warm holiday feeling as they trudged along.

"Thanks for letting us stay, Penny," said Neil. "I've been really looking forward to this break." It would be five days before he and Emily went home on Christmas Eve.

"No problem," replied Penny.

"The film sounds great. Are you going to be in it, too?" Emily asked. Neil and Emily were scheduled to have brief walk-on parts.

"Yes. I'm one of Queen Guinevere's ladies. I have to sit in the background and sew a lot." Penny made a face. "Tons of the locals are extras too."

At the other end of the village, a narrow lane led down to Ainsworth Castle. Snowploughs had heaped snow on either side so high that Neil felt he was walking through a white tunnel. Jake scrabbled excitedly at the frozen walls, but King paced along beside Penny with a more dignified air.

"Doesn't all this snow spoil the filming?" asked Emily as her boots crunched underfoot.

"No, the film is *meant* to be set in winter." Penny's eyes shone. "It's so exciting! They've built a whole village in the clearing beside the lake."

"Cool!" said Neil.

Jake barked his agreement.

Soon they reached Ainsworth Castle, which was built on an island in the lake itself. It was joined to the shore by a short stone causeway leading to an arched gate with a portcullis. Grey towers rose up behind thick walls and scarlet pennants fluttered from the battlements. There couldn't be anywhere better, Neil thought, to be King Arthur's legendary castle Camelot.

"Max said to go straight down to the village," said Penny. "I won't come with you. I promised to help wrap Christmas presents."

"Sure," said Neil. "See you later, then."

Penny went off across the causeway with King. The footpath to the set led off to the right through the woods around the lake shore. By now Jake had run off some of his energy, and was trotting at Neil's heel, only now and again darting away to snuffle in the hollows under the trees.

There were deep ruts in the snow where heavy vehicles had passed, and busy footprints in both directions. Neil and Emily plodded through the slush until they came to the edge of the trees.

Here Neil stopped and pursed his lips in a soundless whistle. "Wow! Just look at that!"

Ahead of them stood a medieval village. Small huts built of wood and interlaced branches were grouped around a central square flanked by bigger buildings. One of them had a sign saying it was an inn. Neil and Emily could see that the buildings weren't real, just front and side walls, all held up at the back with wooden supports and metal scaffolding poles.

On one side of the village were parked several modern trailers, with a group of people in medieval costume standing around drinking tea from plastic cups. On the other side, two or three horses with brightly coloured trappings stood calmly beside their handlers. A knight was mounted on one of them, wearing silver armour and a white surcoat with red diagonal stripes. Film cameras were positioned all round the village, trained on the central area.

As Neil and Emily watched, they heard a sudden spate of barking and a golden cocker spaniel came racing into the village square from behind the inn, his silky ears flying and his long, feathery tail flowing out behind him.

"It's Prince!" said Emily.

Neil bent over, clipped a lead on Jake's collar

and put a hand on the young dog's muzzle to quieten him – just in case he ruined the scene by barking in reply.

As Prince dashed across the square, Max appeared in costume as Zeno, his character in *The Time Travellers*. He was running after Prince, only to slip and fall full length in the snow. Behind him, a knight in black armour appeared on a magnificent black horse, and hurtled towards Max, bending low in the saddle as if he was going to slash him with his sword.

"Oh, no!" Emily whispered. "He'll kill Max!"

As she spoke, a voice yelled, "Cut!" and another man strode out into the square. He was youngish, with fair hair, and was wearing a thick sheepskin jacket with its collar turned up.

"There's Brian Mason," Neil said, recognizing the director of *The Time Travellers*. "What's eating him? The scene looked all right to me."

"Where's Sir Lancelot?" shouted the director.

Max got up and brushed the snow off himself.

Another mounted knight, the one in silver armour, urged his horse forward a few paces into the square. He flicked up his visor. The actor was young and dark-haired, with a bad-tempered expression.

Emily nudged Neil. "That's Brett Benson," she said. "He's Sir Lancelot in the film. He's gorgeous!"

"I'm sorry I missed my cue," Brett Benson said. "But it was this wretched dog – he got in the way of the horse."

"That's not fair!" Neil said hotly. "Prince was nowhere near his horse!" Neil could not help himself – he had to make sure the director did not blame Prince for something he did not do. With Jake in tow he marched across to Brian Mason and the knight, and bent to rumple Prince's ears as the cocker spaniel bounded up, barking excitedly. "Sorry to interrupt, Mr Mason," he said. "I was watching just now and thought Prince was fine." Neil glared up at the mounted knight.

Brett Benson glared back. "Huh! How am I supposed to work when the set's swarming with kids? Where's the proper dog trainer?"

"Here." The woman who spoke was tall and fair-haired, wearing a red puffer jacket. "And this 'kid' is quite right, Brett. Prince *wasn't* in the way."

Brian Mason gave Neil a distracted look. "Oh, hello, Neil." He quickly turned away. "It doesn't matter. Let's go again. Maggie, make sure you

hang on to Prince when he runs over here, eh? Right, folks, places everybody . . . come on, hurry. Brett, you're going to be great."

Brett gave Neil another dirty look, and adjusted his helmet. Max came up, tossed off a "Hi, talk to you in a minute," and went off again with Prince.

Two members of the film crew hurried on to the set from the trailers, to check the actors' costume and make-up ready for the new take.

The fair-haired woman smiled at Neil and Emily and said, "You must be the Parkers. I'm Maggie Brown, the film's dog trainer. From what Max has told me, it sounds as if you're just as keen on dogs as I am!"

Before Neil and Emily could say hello, the barking began again. This time, when Prince dashed across the square, Maggie was waiting to grip him by the collar.

The scene went according to plan and when Max was out of range of the cameras, he relaxed and walked over to join Neil and the others with the dogs. "Thanks for sticking up for Prince. Brett Benson's a real pain."

Emily looked disappointed. "I thought he'd be nice."

"No way." Max sounded angry. "He can't stand it that Prince is the real star of this film. He complains the whole time."

Max squatted down to pat Prince, and the dog licked his face enthusiastically. "You were great, boy," he said, admiring his shining golden coat and his lively, intelligent expression. "By the way, it's great to see you both – and Jake," he added quickly, as the young collie pushed forward, demanding attention. "And I've got news for you . . ."

"What is it?" Emily asked excitedly.

"Something really special." Max sounded mysterious. "But you have to wait until we get back to the castle." He called to the director as he came striding up. "Brian, are we finished?"

"No, sorry," Brian said. "Before the light goes, I want to pick up the scene where you're searching for Sir Kay."

"OK," said Max. He turned to Neil and Emily. "This shouldn't take long. It's just me and Prince."

"Right," said Brian, leading Max back towards the square. Neil and the others followed and waited at the edge of the acting area, where they overheard the director reminding Max of the scene. "Sir Kay went to fight the Black Knight and was captured. You and Prince look for him, and Prince finds him wounded inside the inn. He barks to you out of the window, and you go in. Have you got that?"

Max nodded.

"We'll rehearse it once," said Brian, "and then we'll go for a take."

Maggie strode across the village square and into the inn, ready to make sure that Prince barked on cue. Max and Prince both vanished around a corner.

Moments later, the crew settled down and Brian called, "Action!"

Prince reappeared, sniffing his way across

the square until he pawed at the inn door. It swung open, and Prince went in. Now Zeno came cautiously out of the doorway opposite, peered through the window of the next house, and moved on.

A camera running alongside him on tracks followed his progress.

The shutters of one of the inn windows were pushed open. Prince had his front paws up on the sill and let out a sharp bark. Zeno looked up. Then, as Prince barked again, the sound was drowned out by a sudden crash and a splintering noise as the roof of the inn sagged inwards.

Max yelled, "Prince!" and started to run.

Prince scrabbled at the sill as if he was trying to climb out. Then he vanished as the walls started to tilt crazily like a collapsing house of cards.

"It's falling apart!" Neil exclaimed from his vantage point nearby. "Prince will be trapped!"

Chapter Two

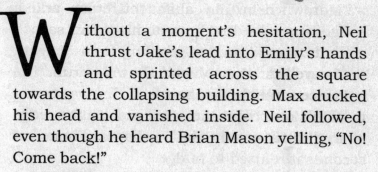

Without a moment's hesitation, Neil thrust Jake's lead into Emily's hands and sprinted across the square towards the collapsing building. Max ducked his head and vanished inside. Neil followed, even though he heard Brian Mason yelling, "No! Come back!"

Inside the air was thick with dust. Blinking as it stung his eyes, Neil saw that some of the scaffolding poles had collapsed and Max was trying to climb over them.

"Prince is here somewhere," he gasped when he saw Neil. "But I can't see him. Or Maggie."

Neil couldn't see them either. In the far corner was a wooden staircase leading up to the window where Prince had appeared. It looked as if some of the steps had given way and pulled the outer wall down with them. The scaffolding had shifted so that it wasn't holding up the roof properly. The roof was tilted inwards, half-covering the remains of the stairs.

Neil thought Prince and Maggie must be somewhere underneath. He could still hear Brian yelling at him from outside, but he took no notice. Scrambling over the scaffolding poles, he reached the sagging roof.

"Max – help me shift this!" he yelled, coughing as the dust got into his throat.

There was a sudden whining from beneath the board, and then Maggie Brown's voice. "I've got Prince. We're OK, I think . . . "

With Max beside him, Neil grabbed the edge of the board and heaved upwards. For a few seconds it refused to budge.

"It's caught on something," Max said, trying to get his shoulder underneath.

Neil and Max hauled on the roof again. Suddenly Neil realized there was someone else beside them, helping to take the weight. The roof swung upwards and Maggie Brown, bent almost double, stumbled out, pushing Prince in front of her.

The man beside Neil let go of the roof, grabbed Prince by the collar and dragged him through the gap at the back of the building. Maggie followed him as Neil and Max let the roof drop. Neil staggered, off-balance, as it crashed down, and wrapped his arms around his head to protect himself from a rain of debris.

Just as Neil clutched Max's arm and pulled his friend to safety, he heard a soft crunching sound, and behind him the whole of the village inn folded and settled into a heap of wreckage.

Maggie Brown was kneeling on the ground outside, trying to get her breath. The other man was still holding Prince. Weak with relief, Neil

staggered towards them. "Thanks!" he gasped. "That was great! Are you all right?"

The man let Prince go and straightened up. He had thinning dark hair and a straggly beard, and he wore the drab tunic and leggings of a medieval peasant. His face was smeared with make-up and dust.

"No problem," he said abruptly. "I think the dog's OK."

Before Neil could reply, Emily came dashing up, along with Jake and a tall, dark-haired young woman. Neil recognized Suzie, Max's chaperone, who had to be on set when he was filming. Right now she looked furious.

"Do you know what might have happened?" she said to Neil. "You and Max could have been killed!"

"We had to save Prince," Max said, falling to his knees beside his beloved dog and running his hands over him to check for injuries. "Thanks, Neil, you were great."

"It wasn't me," Neil started to explain. "It was . . . " He looked round, but the peasant had disappeared. "Hey, where did he go?"

"I didn't see him leave – but I'm so grateful to him. Maybe he was one of the extras," said Max. "Tell me if you see him, Neil. I want to thank him. I don't think Prince is hurt at all."

"What happened?" Emily asked. "What made it collapse like that?"

By now Maggie had recovered, and was helping Max to examine Prince. "I don't know," she said. "I was waiting inside ready for Prince to come down from the window. When I put my weight on the steps they gave way, and then the whole lot started to come down."

"Are you all right, Maggie?" asked Brian Mason, approaching and peering at Prince over Max's shoulder.

"Bruised, that's all," said Maggie with a smile. "It's Prince I'm worried about."

Prince was standing quietly; the shock had subdued his usual boisterous nature. Neil guessed that would soon wear off and the cocker spaniel didn't seem to be physically injured.

"We'd better get the vet to check him out," said Brian. "Go up to the castle and give him a ring." He gestured towards the ruins of the inn. "Now we'll be held up again until this is fixed. Honestly, sometimes I think there's a jinx on this film."

Neil and the others headed for the castle. Flakes of snow started to drift down and quickly grew into thick flurries that were swept across the path by the wind. Neil hunched his shoulders and buried his hands deep in his pockets.

"Max," he asked, "what did Brian mean – about a jinx on the film?"

Max frowned, looking worried. "This isn't the first accident," he said. "A couple of days ago one of the horses went berserk when he had a scene with Prince. Prince was nearly trampled, weren't you, boy? And then on another day part of my costume went missing and turned up in Prince's basket! Brian thought he'd dragged it in there, but I know he didn't."

"Prince would never do anything like that," said Emily.

Daylight was beginning to fade as they reached the open space in front of Ainsworth Castle. The snow shone eerily in the dying light. Neil tramped thankfully across the causeway, looking forward to a hot drink and something to eat.

The arched gateway led into a courtyard. The main entrance to the castle was at the top of a flight of steps opposite, through a pair of thick wooden doors studded with iron nails. Neil and the others stood stamping snow off

142

their boots in the hallway, while Jake shook himself and showered everybody with icy drops. Maggie disappeared, saying she would phone the vet.

"Max, you told us you had some news," Emily said.

"Yes," said Neil, stripping off his jacket. "And we had to wait for it until we got back to the castle. So come on, what is it?"

Max started to smile, his worried look vanishing. "You'll really like this," he promised. "Won't they, Prince?"

Prince barked in agreement.

"I'll have to find Adrian," Max went on. "He said he'd help while I'm on set."

Max pulled open the doors to the Great Hall and went inside; Neil followed him, giving Emily a puzzled look, wondering what Adrian Bartlett, Lord Ainsworth's steward, had to do with Max's secret. Then he stood still, gaping. "Wow!" he exclaimed.

Neil had been in the hall of Ainsworth Castle before, but he had never seen it like this. Tapestries covered the walls. Iron sconces holding torches were fixed to the pillars. Over the enormous fireplace at the far end brightly painted shields were hanging. A huge round table stood in the middle, surrounded by carved wooden seats.

"King Arthur's Great Hall," Max said.

Neil could easily imagine armoured knights coming to sit in council round the table. It took him a minute to notice the lights fixed high in the roof, and remember that this was a film set.

"It's wonderful!" said Emily. "It looks so authentic!"

In front of the fireplace were two people Neil recognized; Jeff Calton, the producer of *The Time Travellers*, and Adrian Bartlett. Adrian was a smallish man with fair hair and a thin, beaky face. He broke off what he was saying to Jeff as Neil and the others came in.

"Hello," he said, smiling. "Welcome to Camelot."

"Adrian," said Max, "where's . . . you know?"

Adrian's eyes twinkled. "Over here."

He beckoned them towards King Arthur's Round Table, and the massive carved chair where the king himself would sit. As Neil came closer, he saw a tiny head looking up from the chair's velvet cushion. A silky golden head, with soft, floppy ears and huge brown eyes. One silky paw was dangling over the edge. The little pup stirred and let out a high-pitched yap.

Prince went to stand beside the chair, and looked up at the miniature of himself, whining softly.

Max's grin was wide enough to split his face. "Meet Princess," he said.

Chapter Three

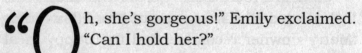

"Oh, she's gorgeous!" Emily exclaimed. "Can I hold her?"

Max carefully lifted the cocker spaniel pup, and Emily cuddled her with a blissful smile on her face.

"Where did you get her?" Neil asked. "And why didn't you tell us?"

"She's Prince's daughter," Max said. He looked a bit embarrassed. "We were on holiday this summer in a cottage in Wales, and some people down the road had a cocker spaniel bitch called Merry. She and Prince got together before anybody knew about it."

Emily giggled. "Prince, you naughty dog!"

"They were all good pups," Max went on, "and

146

Merry's owner was pleased in the end. I didn't tell you before, because I wasn't sure if I could have Princess. I've only just got her – she's my Christmas present from Mum and Dad."

"She's a *great* present," said Emily. She held Princess close and stroked her head. "You're going to be a star just like your dad!"

Princess gave a sharp little yap as if she agreed, and swiped her tongue over Emily's face.

"She's a star already," said Max.

"What are you feeding her?" Neil asked.

"I wanted to ask you about that," Max said. "Merry's owner recommended the puppy meal that she uses, but it looks a bit boring to me. What can I give Princess to make her meals more interesting?"

"You need the Puppy Patrol advice service, mate," Neil said. He always had all the latest dog care facts at his fingertips. "How old is she?"

"Twelve weeks."

"Well, when Jake was a young pup I used to give him cereal and milk for variety. Then you could start adding in just a little bit of meat, with some rice, or maybe pasta—"

"Hey, I'm not running a restaurant!" said Max, laughing.

Jake tentatively approached the chair and sniffed the young spaniel pup. Princess drew back initially, then yapped and welcomed the Border collie to her castle with a brief touching of their black button noses.

Everybody laughed.

"Plenty of fresh drinking water too," Neil went on, "but you know that anyway. And not too many treats, because—"

Before he could finish, Jeff Calton, who had been scribbling notes on a clipboard, came up and said, "What's the matter? You two are filthy! And Prince!"

Max explained about the collapsing village inn, and how he and Neil had rescued Prince. "Maggie's gone to phone the vet to get him to check Prince out," he finished.

As he was speaking, Jeff had begun to look more and more angry. "I've had enough of this!" he said. "The film can't stand further delays. Now I'll have to talk to Brian and get those scenes rescheduled. I'll have a few words to say to the set builders, too."

He strode off. Then Adrian said, "I'd better let Lord Ainsworth know as well," and followed him.

Max was starting to look worried again. Hoping to take his friend's mind off his

148

problems, Neil asked, "So what's this film all about?"

"Well," Max explained, "Zeno and Prince get carried back through the time tunnel to the court of King Arthur. They meet the witch queen Morgan le Fay, and she steals the time tunnel controller, so Zeno can't get away. Morgan wants to kill King Arthur and make herself High Queen, so Zeno and Prince help Arthur to defeat her."

"Sounds great," Neil said.

"But just a minute," Emily objected. "King Arthur's a legend. He wasn't real, was he? I mean, not like this, with a castle and knights and a Round Table. So how can Zeno get into his time?"

Max shrugged and grinned. "Don't ask me, ask the scriptwriters!"

While Max changed out of costume, Neil and Emily phoned their mum and dad to tell them they'd arrived safely. Carole Parker answered the phone.

"How was your journey?" she asked when Emily had poured out all the news about Princess. "The TV news said there was snow up there."

"Lots of it!" said Neil. "Listen, Mum, there's something I forgot to say. Keep Squirt out of my bedroom, will you? I've hidden all your Christmas presents in there."

"*Sarah* is teaching Fudge to sing 'Jingle Bells'. I think that will keep her occupied over the next few days."

Neil laughed. His little sister, Sarah, thought that Fudge, her hamster, was clever enough to do anything. "That's just like Squirt!" he said, still laughing as he said goodbye and put the phone down.

Neil woke next morning to find that Jake had sprung up onto his bed and started to lick his face. "Get off, trouble!" he said, pushing Jake gently to one side and sitting up.

The bedroom was cold and dark – Ainsworth Castle had no central heating – and when Neil squinted at the clock on the bedside table he saw that it was still only seven. He would have liked to crawl back under the warm blankets and sleep for another hour, but as soon as Jake saw he had succeeded in waking up his owner the young dog leapt off the bed and started to paw at the door.

"OK, boy," Neil said, sighing heavily. "You

win! Walk before breakfast."

He had a quick wash and pulled on warm clothes and boots. Before he had finished getting ready, his door burst open and Emily came in.

"There was more snow in the night," she said excitedly. "D'you think the road to the village will be blocked? We might be cut off!"

Neil stifled a yawn. "Shouldn't think so. Coming for a walk?"

With Jake pattering behind, they went down the back staircase and along the passage past the kitchens which led into the courtyard. Even here they could see how the film crew had taken over the castle. Lighting equipment was stacked in a storeroom just inside the side door, and across the passage the old castle scullery had been transformed into a make-up room, with stage make-up strewn over tables and lines of chairs facing mirrors propped against the wall.

A girl was there, touching up the make-up of one of the cast. Neil caught a glimpse of the man's face in the mirror as he walked past. It was the extra who had helped Prince when the set collapsed the day before. The girl was loading some filthy gunge onto his face.

"Hello," Neil said, stopping in the doorway. "Wasn't it you who—"

The make-up girl jumped at the sound of his voice. "Do you mind?" she said irritably. "There are people here trying to concentrate."

She flounced across the room and slammed the door in Neil's face.

Neil gaped. "What did I say?"

"You startled her," Emily said. "Maybe she just doesn't like people watching her work."

Neil shrugged. He'd only wanted to thank the man for helping Prince. Still, he told himself, maybe anybody would be feeling snappy if they had to start work at this time in the morning.

He followed Emily into the courtyard, where they met Max with Prince, and Princess tucked into the front of his padded jacket.

"I thought we'd be the first ones up," said Neil.

Max laughed and shook his head. "Not on a film set! Every day's an early start."

"Yes," said Emily. "There's someone in make-up already."

"They'll want me soon," said Max, "but I've just got time to walk Prince."

Together they crossed the causeway and took the footpath that led to the lake.

Where the path curved down to the water's edge, more early risers had gathered. Neil didn't recognize some of them but he assumed they were actors in the film. Looking out onto the lake, he saw Penny, with Adrian Bartlett, skimming along expertly on ice skates. She raised a hand to wave as she glided past.

"I'd like to do that," Emily said. "Do you think Penny would teach me?"

"Suppose so," said Neil. "Better be careful, though."

"The ice is safe enough for now," Lord Ainsworth said. He was standing beside the lake with King, watching the skaters. "I tested it myself, first thing."

Even so, Neil wasn't sure he fancied ice skating. He carried on around the lake, with Emily and Max, while Jake and Prince played together, chasing each other and plunging through the fresh, powdery snow. Prince was his usual lively self. Max reported that the vet from Beckthwaite, David Blackburn, had checked him over the night before and found no injuries from his accident.

"Neil," Max said, "do you reckon it's OK to let Princess run around? It won't be too cold for her in all this snow?"

"Well, she can't stay inside your jacket all day," Neil said, laughing. "She'll be fine if you don't keep her out for too long. And make sure you give her a good towelling when we get back."

Max put the wriggling Princess down in the snow. She sniffed at it and sneezed, and then took off after her dad and Jake, her feathery tail waving and her long ears bouncing up and down. Excited little yaps came from her as she ran.

Neil shook his head. "You've got your work cut out there!"

Further along the lake, Neil caught sight of Maggie Brown, walking back towards the castle with an enormous dog at her side. He grabbed Emily's arm. "Hey, there's Fred!"

As he spoke, the dog gave a welcoming bark and began loping ahead of the trainer. He was

huge, with a rough grey coat and a long tail which waved enthusiastically as he came up to Neil. Neil rumpled his ears and fished in his pocket for a dog treat. "Hi, Fred," he said. "What's it like being a movie star?"

Fred was an Irish wolfhound who had taken part in the *Time Travellers* episode filmed at Padsham Castle near Neil's home at King Street Kennels. He'd been such a hit as another heroic knight's war hound that Jeff Calton had asked for him again, to play the part of King Arthur's favourite hound, Cabal.

"He loves it," Maggie said as she caught up. "Bill had to go home, but Fred doesn't seem to be missing him too much."

Bill Grey, Fred's owner, kept a butcher's shop in Padsham, and the few days before Christmas were the busiest in the year for him.

"If you like, I'll help—" Neil began, and then broke off. Out of the corner of his eye he had seen Jake dash out onto the frozen lake. Neil spun round to see him darting in and out of the group of skaters, with Prince on his heels, barking madly, and Princess doing her best to keep up.

Max laughed as Brett Benson tripped over

Prince and only just managed to right himself and avoid falling flat on his back.

"Jake! Jake!" Neil yelled.

"They're OK," Max said. "They're only playing."

But in his mind Neil could see a yawning gap open up in the ice, and his beloved dog sliding helplessly into dark water. He couldn't help remembering the day Sam died, when Jake had been carried away in the river.

Jake would have drowned that day if it had not been for Sam. He'd given his own life as his damaged heart failed in the fight to pull Jake to safety. Part of Neil knew he was being stupid, but he could see the whole horrible accident happening again.

"Jake! Here!" he yelled.

Out on the ice, Jake stopped, ears cocked. Prince dashed up to him and playfully hurled himself on top of the young Border collie; the two dogs rolled over and over together.

"Jake! Come here!"

Neil knew that he ought to go and grab Jake, but when he thought about putting his weight onto the ice he felt sick. Even though he could see it was thick enough to bear lots of other people, he still couldn't help imagining it splintering, plunging him into the lake.

He was taking a breath to shout again when Jake got to his feet, shook himself, and began trotting obediently to the bank. As soon as Neil could grip his collar without venturing onto the ice, he clipped on his lead. "Heel, Jake. Now!"

He realized that Max was staring at him. "Hey, Neil, it's not . . ."

Neil took no notice. Then he heard Emily say under her breath, "Don't bother him, Max. It's because of what happened to Jake when Sam died. He nearly drowned, and so did Neil."

It was no help to Neil to realize that Emily understood. He felt hot and uncomfortable, as if he'd been caught doing something he shouldn't.

It was worse still when Max asked, "Neil, are you afraid of water now? Because—"

"I don't want to talk about it, OK?" Neil snapped.

He pulled at Jake's lead, and started to run along the path to the castle. As he was going he heard Emily say, "I think you're right, Max. He'll have to get over it, but it might take a long time."

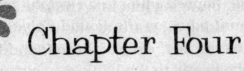

Chapter Four

"**W**hat do you want from me?" said King Arthur. "Speak."

The king and his noble knights were seated around the Round Table in the Great Hall at Camelot. Zeno walked forward from the doorway, with his faithful dog at his heels, and bowed low to the king.

"My Lord Arthur," he said, "Queen Morgan le Fay has stolen something valuable from me. I need your help to get it back."

King Arthur gravely stroked his beard, while Sir Kay, his steward, leaned closer to him and said, "My lord, how do we know this boy isn't a spy from Morgan?"

As he spoke, Prince bounded down the length

of the hall, hopped up onto an empty seat and put his front paws on the Round Table to bark indignantly at Sir Kay. The other knights laughed.

"Prince is so cool!" Neil murmured.

Along with Emily and Penny, he was sitting in the minstrels' gallery above the hall, watching the scene that was being shot below. He never stopped being amazed at how perfectly trained Prince was, and how he always seemed to know what he was supposed to do.

"And look at Fred!" said Emily, pointing at the huge wolfhound sprawled lazily in front of the fireplace. "He's pretty good, too."

Down below, Sir Lancelot was rising to his feet, but instead of getting on with the scene, he looked round for Brian Mason, and said, "Brian, I don't think this scene is right."

"Cut!" Brian yelled at the camera crew. "What's the matter now, Brett?"

"Well, everybody knows that Sir Lancelot was Arthur's best knight," said Brett Benson. "I reckon I should have a line there, instead of the stupid business with the dog."

Brian Mason banged down his clipboard. Some of the knights started to mutter among themselves. The actor playing Sir Kay put his chin on his hands and said, "Here we go again!"

"Brett," said Brian, "I thought up that 'stupid business' with the dog, along with Maggie Brown and the scriptwriters. Can't you understand that in this film it's the dog who's the star?"

Brett Benson looked furious. "Then if the dog's the star, you obviously don't need an actor of my talents. Find yourself another Sir Lancelot!"

His chair scraped on the flagstones as he pushed it back and marched out of the hall. Brian Mason took a deep breath, called, "OK, folks, take five!" and hurried after him.

"Oh, no!" said Emily. "They've stopped filming again. They're never going to finish at this rate."

"I'm going down to talk to Max," said Neil.

With Emily and Penny following, he ran down the steps from the gallery and into the hall. Max was standing near the fireplace, talking to Suzie and Maggie Brown, but when he saw Neil and the others he came to meet them, with Prince trotting beside him.

Neil could see that Max was seething with fury.

"That was a really good take, until he ruined it!" fumed Max.

"Take it easy," Neil said. "It'll be just as good next time."

Prince made a soft whining sound and pushed his nose into Max's hand. Max relaxed a bit and stroked his head.

"Why don't you get another Sir Lancelot if Brett Benson is such a pain?" Penny asked.

"I wish we could!" Max said. "But that would mean repeating all the scenes we've already shot. It would cost far too much, and Brett Benson knows it."

"And I used to be a fan of his!" Emily said indignantly.

"What really gets me," Max went on, "is that he doesn't care about the *film* at all. He only cares about Brett Benson. Honestly, if he—"

A voice interrupted him, shouting loudly from the passage outside. "Max! Where's Max got to? Max!"

Neil turned round. In the hall doorway stood Jeff Calton. His hair was untidy and his face was red with anger. He had a sheaf of tattered papers in one hand, and in the other, held by the scruff of the neck, was Princess. A shred of

161

white paper was dangling from the little pup's jaws.

Princess was whimpering. Max stormed over to Jeff Calton and took her away from him. "Don't hold her like that! You're hurting her!"

"Then look after her properly!" Jeff yelled back at him. "Look what she's done!"

He brandished the papers in Max's face. Max took a step back, holding Princess close to him. "These are my production notes. They're vital. Now I'll have to do the whole lot again because your puppy chewed them up."

Neil came to stand beside Max. Princess was trembling, and trying to hide her head in the crook of Max's arm.

"Hang on a minute," Neil said. "Everybody knows that pups chew things. If you left your notes lying around, Mr Calton, you're just as much to blame as Princess."

Jeff Calton stared at him as if he didn't remember who he was. "Those notes were left in a file in my bedroom," he snapped. "With the door closed."

"Then how did Princess get at them?" Max asked.

"How should I know? When I went up there just now, she was in the middle of the floor making a meal of them. You simply can't have her here, Max, if you can't take better care of her than that."

Max went red at the suggestion that he couldn't take care of his dog. His hand shaking, he stroked Princess and said nothing.

"It's not Max's fault," Emily said, coming to stick up for him. "He was on set."

"Then who was supposed to be looking after the dog?"

"Adrian," said Penny. "He offered to look after Princess and Jake."

Neil began to think he understood. Adrian Bartlett was a whizz at taking charge of Lord Ainsworth's business affairs, but a bit vague about everything else. Princess might well have wandered away from him, but that still didn't explain how she managed to get into Jeff Calton's bedroom, or open the file.

"So where is Adrian now?" Jeff asked.

Adrian Bartlett himself answered the question by walking through the doors as Jeff was speaking. He wore his outdoor clothes, and had Jake on a lead. He smiled at Neil as he handed the young dog over, stamped his feet on the floor to warm them up, and asked, "Is there a problem?"

Jeff launched into a long complaint about his ruined notes.

"I'm terribly sorry," Adrian said when he had finished. "Jake needed a walk, and Princess was asleep in her basket in the kitchen, so I left her there. We were only gone twenty minutes or so."

"And you remembered to shut the door, I suppose?" Jeff said sarcastically, not waiting for an answer. "I've had just about enough of this," he went on. "I'm going to phone Manchester and get a couple more security staff sent down. From now on, nothing's going to happen round here unless I say so."

He spun round, but his dramatic exit was spoilt when he nearly tripped over Jake, who barked in protest as he darted to one side.

"Dogs!" Jeff Calton snarled. "I've had dogs up to here!"

He strode out.

Adrian looked after him with a bewildered expression. "I did shut the door," he said. "I don't know how she managed to get out."

"It's not your fault," Penny said loyally. "He must have left the notes lying around, whatever he says."

But Neil wasn't so sure. He knew how

efficient Jeff Calton was. "Max, you know what you told us, about the accidents?"

"You've been pretty unlucky, haven't you?" Emily added.

"Well, yes . . ." said Max.

"It's just . . ." Neil began. He paused as he put two and two together and came up with an answer he didn't like at all. "Well, what if they're not accidents?"

"What do you mean?" asked Penny.

"I mean that they're happening too often. It just can't be coincidence. It's almost as if somebody is doing it on purpose."

"They couldn't be." Max had gone pale.

"Oh, yes, they could," said Neil. "How do you think Princess managed to get into Jeff Calton's room, unless somebody put her there? How do you think she got the notes out of the file all by herself? Max . . ." He hesitated and then went on, "Max, can you think of anyone who would deliberately try to wreck this film?"

Chapter Five

N eil halted and stood panting, watching his breath puff out into the cold air. "Whew!" he gasped. "These branches are heavy!"

After the scene in the Great Hall was eventually finished, he and Emily had gone into the woods with the dogs to cut greenery for Christmas decorations. Now they were pulling a sledge back to the castle, loaded with holly and yew boughs and trailing strands of ivy.

Jake and Prince were frolicking about among the trees, and Princess sat in the middle of the branches, looking as proud as if she was riding in a royal coach. Neil was looking after the dogs for Max, so that Max could shut himself up in

his bedroom and learn some lines for the following day.

Emily laughed, and picked up the sledge rope that Neil had dropped. "Medieval peasants had to collect wood every day, you know."

"Well, I'm glad I'm not a medieval peasant then," Neil said, rubbing his aching back.

"But you're going to be," Emily said. "Max told me. Just as soon as they rebuild the village."

"Why am I always a peasant?" Neil complained. "Why don't I get to be a knight, or even a squire?"

"Or a huntsman with the hounds," Emily teased.

Neil brightened up. "Yeah! That'd be ace!"

"Come on," said Emily. "Let's get back before we freeze. I'll pull for a bit."

As they began slogging through the snow again, Emily asked, "Neil, are you really convinced that somebody's trying to spoil the filming?"

"Yes, I am."

"But who would do that?"

His sister didn't sound as if she expected an answer, but Neil gave her one. "I think it might be Brett Benson."

"Oh, him!" Emily sniffed. "I wouldn't be surprised. But if the film isn't made, he'll be out of a job."

Neil watched his feet crunching into the snow, as if that would help him concentrate. "I didn't want to say this in front of Max, but most of the things that have gone wrong involve the dogs – Prince mostly, and now Princess as well. And who around here can't stand Prince?"

"Brett Benson!" said Emily.

"Right. Maybe he thinks that if he causes enough trouble, Prince will be out of the film and he'll be the star."

"But that doesn't make sense! It's a *Time Travellers* film. Prince has to be in it."

"You know that. I know that. The whole world and his dog knows that," Neil said. "But does Brett Benson know it? He doesn't act like he does. I reckon he keeps delaying the filming, just because—"

Neil broke off as he heard frantic barking from among the trees where the dogs had been playing. Princess started yapping in reply.

"That sounds like Prince!" Neil said. "I wonder what's wrong. Em, keep an eye on Princess."

He left the path and plunged into the snow under the trees. "Prince! Prince, here, boy!"

The cocker spaniel came dashing out from behind a bramble thicket, snow spraying from his paws as he hurtled along. When he saw Neil he stopped barking, ran to meet him, and stood panting and trembling by his side.

Neil reached down and ruffled his fur. "What's the matter, boy?"

Emily dropped the sledge rope and came to look. "Maybe he's cut one of his paws, or picked up a thorn," she suggested.

"He wasn't limping," Neil replied. He ran a hand down Prince's flank. The spaniel was standing quietly now, and seemed to be settling down. Neil was mystified. "I'll take a look." He began to retrace Prince's tracks through the snow.

He had started to worry about where Jake

was, but as he skirted the bramble thicket he heard the young collie barking playfully. When Jake came into sight he was bounding around a figure in medieval costume who was holding a branch up for Jake to leap and snap at. Neil recognized the extra who had helped Prince when the village inn collapsed.

"Hi!" he called. "Did you see what—"

The extra turned, saw him, threw the branch down, and ran off through the trees. Jake gave a bark of protest that his game had ended so abruptly, then pounced on the branch and held it up for Neil. Neil squatted down to rub his head. "OK, boy?" he said. "Weird, or what?"

The extra couldn't have done anything to hurt Prince or Jake wouldn't have played so happily with him. But something had upset the cocker spaniel. Neil wished the man had stayed so he could have asked what it was.

He straightened up, and went back to where Prince and the others were waiting for him. Jake trotted along beside him. "I wish you could talk, boy," Neil said. "Maybe you could make some sense out of what's going on around here."

*

By the following morning the repairs to the damaged building were finished, so filming could start again in the village. Jeff Calton sent Neil and Emily to the wardrobe mistress to be fitted out with peasant costumes.

"The wardrobe is in a room off the Long Gallery," Max explained, as he led the way up the spiral staircase. Prince was with him, and he was carrying Princess tucked into the crook of his arm. The cocker spaniel pup was too small to keep up with them on the stairs, but Neil thought Max was secretly pleased to have an excuse for giving her a cuddle.

Prince had completely recovered from whatever had spooked him in the woods, and was his usual cheerful self, bounding ahead of Max up the stairs. Neil had left Jake with Maggie Brown – he didn't feel confident that the excitable young dog would behave himself amongst all the costumes.

As they reached the top of the stairs, they almost cannoned into Adrian Bartlett, who was hurrying along in the other direction.

"Adrian," said Max, "would you mind keeping an eye on Princess again? I've got to go down to the village set."

"What?" Adrian was looking hot and

bothered, as if he had something else on his mind. "Oh – Princess. Yes, of course, Max. Shall I take her now?"

"Please." Max handed Princess over, and the little dog put her paws on Adrian's chest and licked his face enthusiastically, dislodging his glasses. "She likes you," said Max.

"Er . . . yes." Adrian gave Max a distracted smile, and darted off down the stairs, carrying Princess.

"What's bugging him?" said Neil.

Nobody answered.

The Long Gallery was a wide corridor on the first floor of Ainsworth Castle. On one side, windows looked out over the lake. Rooms led off the other side and through one open door, Neil saw props and coats of armour for the film – helmets and swords and shields and a whole rack of chainmail tunics.

Hanging on the gallery walls were huge paintings in heavy gold frames. Neil lagged behind to look at them. Most were portraits of men and women in old-fashioned dress, and featured dogs which looked just like King. Neil remembered that for hundreds of years King's line of Great Danes had been the special companions of the Ainsworth family.

Just then he heard Emily calling to him from further down the gallery. "Come on, Neil, we're waiting for you!"

Neil hurried along to join her at the door of a larger room at the far end. One wall was lined with costumes, and at the other side there was a sewing machine and ironing board, and screens for the cast to change behind. Max was just disappearing with his Zeno costume, and Prince sat quietly down to wait for him as people rushed in and out of the changing area.

Brett Benson was also there, wearing a blue velvet tunic with long scalloped sleeves, and smirking at himself in a mirror.

"This belt's wrong," he said. "Find me another, Verity."

The wardrobe mistress stopped sorting among the costumes on the rack. She was a slender young woman with short, dark curls. She had a friendly smile for Neil and Emily, but she sounded exasperated as she said, "OK, Brett. Just as soon as I've kitted out these peasants."

Brett swung round, looking bad-tempered. "Why do I have to wait for these kids?"

"Because they're due on set," Verity said patiently. "You're not." She ignored Brett's snort of annoyance as she held up a mud-coloured dress in front of Emily. "That looks about right. Sorry it's not very exciting. Now you," she went on, sizing up Neil with a practised eye. "I reckon I've got—"

"Verity," a voice from the doorway interrupted her, "is my costume ready?"

Verity ran her hands through her curls. The woman who had spoken was tall and striking, with long, dark hair and a pale, haughty-looking face.

"That's Morgan le Fay," Emily murmured to Neil. "The evil enchantress."

Neil nodded.

"You were going to take the seam in," Morgan reminded Verity. "Did you have time to do it? Jeff wants to shoot that scene today."

"Yes, I did it." Verity had begin to hunt along the rack, rattling the hangers along the rails as she searched. "That's funny. I'm sure I put it here."

Neil glanced at Emily, remembering how Max had told them that part of his costume had disappeared. Brett Benson said nastily, "Lost something *again*, Verity dear?"

Neil saw Verity turn pink and start sorting through the costumes even faster. Then she stooped over a pile of black material on the floor. "Here it is. It must have slipped off the hanger."

She stood up with the dress in her hands and shook it out. Morgan gasped. Emily exclaimed, "Oh, no!"

The dress was long and flowing, made of a lot of separate layers of filmy fabric. The top layer was sewn with hundreds of tiny sequins. Neil could imagine it would make a stunning costume for a witch queen, except that all down the front of it were splashes of silver paint.

Verity was staring at the dress; she looked as if she was going to start crying. "I don't believe it. I just don't believe it!" she gasped.

Morgan went up to the dress and dabbed cautiously at the paint marks. "It's not dry yet," she said. "It can't be long since it was done. Verity, is there anything in here that could have got spilt?"

"No," said Verity. "What would I want with paint? It looks like the stuff the props people are using for the armour."

Neil spotted some splashes of paint on the floor where the dress had been, and then got down on hands and knees to look under the costume rack. Catching sight of something in the shadows by the wall, he burrowed underneath and came out with a paint tin in one hand. It was nearly empty, and it had sticky silver dribbles on the outside.

"Is this it?"

Both the women looked at it, and Verity said, "It must be. But how did it get under there?"

"Have you been in here all morning?" Neil asked.

Verity looked flustered, as if she was trying to remember. "I came up after breakfast, and then I went back to my bedroom to fetch some sewing things . . . It could have happened then, I suppose."

"What could have happened?" It was Jeff

176

Calton's voice; the producer was standing in the doorway. "Where are my peasants? We need to— Oh, good grief, just look at that!"

He had caught sight of the dress, which Verity was still holding up. Striding into the room, he examined the paint marks, and let out a long sigh, as if he could barely keep control of his temper. "OK, Verity," he said quietly, "see if it can be cleaned. I'll reschedule the scene. Neil, Emily, get changed and down to the village set right away. Max . . . Where's Max?"

"Here," said Max, emerging from behind the screens in his Zeno costume. As if he couldn't help himself, he added, "At least nobody can blame this on Prince or Princess."

"I wouldn't be too sure," Brett Benson said. He had been lounging against the wall beside the mirror, watching everything with a spiteful smile on his face. Now he came forward and bent over Prince.

Prince backed away, but Brett Benson grabbed him and rubbed some of the feathery hairs on Prince's legs between his finger and thumb. When he showed his hand to Jeff Calton, there were silver marks on it.

"If Prince had nothing to do with it," he said, "then why is there paint on him?"

Chapter Six

Max pushed himself between Brett Benson and his dog. "Leave Prince alone!"

He squatted down and put an arm around Prince's neck. Neil stooped beside him and examined the cocker spaniel's coat. Brett Benson was right – there were flecks of silver paint around Prince's front paws.

Jeff Calton ran a hand through his hair. "Honestly, Max, it's just one thing after another. Can't you keep your dogs under control?"

"Obviously not," said Brett Benson. "But if you will have kids and dogs larking around on set, what can you expect?"

He cast another glance at himself in the

mirror, and strolled out into the gallery, still smirking.

"Prince *is* under control!" Max said hotly. "He didn't spill the paint. I know he didn't!"

"Then how did it get on him?" Jeff asked.

"I don't know!"

"Listen, Mr Calton," Neil said. He was finding it easier than Max to keep calm. After all, it wasn't his dog in trouble. "Just think about it. Verity says the props people are using this paint. Do you think Prince went into the props room, found the paint and carried it along here, just so he could spill it on a costume? And then hid the paint pot under the rack? It's just not possible. It doesn't make sense."

"I don't know what makes sense any more," Jeff said, exasperated. "I just know that this film will be ruined if there's any more trouble. Anyway, Max, and you two – village set in fifteen minutes, OK?"

He strode out. Morgan gave Verity a quick hug and said, "Don't worry," before following him. Emily went behind the screens to change, while Verity put the ruined dress to one side and went back to looking for Neil's costume.

"Max," Neil said while he waited, "where was

Prince this morning? Has he got an alibi for this?"

Max frowned, thinking. "I'm not sure. I fed him in the kitchen first thing, and then I left him there while I went into breakfast. I suppose he could have wandered up here."

"But he didn't fetch the paint from the props room," Neil said. "Somebody else did. Then they spilt the paint on the dress and dabbed some on Prince so that he would get the blame."

Max was looking even more upset now. He was still kneeling beside Prince, an arm around him. "I'm not taking my eyes off Prince after this," he said. "Whoever it is, they'd better not try anything else!"

He straightened up. "Neil, I'm going down to make-up. I'll see you on set. Come on, Prince." He slapped his leg, and Prince trotted obediently after him.

Neil watched him go, and then realized that Verity was holding out his costume: a pair of loose brown trousers and a shirt, with a sheepskin jerkin to go on top.

"Thanks," he said absent-mindedly. As he went off to change he was still thinking about the attempts to sabotage the film, and whether there was anything he could do to put a stop to them.

The collapsed inn had been repaired, and the village looked very realistic under its coating of snow. Brian Mason wanted to film one of the most important scenes of the film, when the villagers, who had been forced to work for the wicked Morgan le Fay, rebelled, joining King Arthur and his knights in an attack on her castle.

"You can't have found *another* castle for Morgan?" Neil said to Max.

"No, it's just a different bit of this one," Max explained. He still sounded tense, and he kept Prince very close beside him while they waited for filming to begin. "But it'll look fine on the film."

Nearby, King Arthur and his knights were mounting their horses, getting ready for the moment when they were to come trotting into the village. The villagers had to cheer them and then listen while Arthur rallied them to fight against the wicked Morgan.

The director called the extras together and explained how the scene would work. While he was talking, Neil noticed the mysterious extra standing at the back of the crowd, head down, as if he didn't want to be seen. Neil edged his way towards him.

"Hi," he said. "Thanks for getting Prince out the other day."

The man gave him a sideways glance, and just grunted. Neil tried not to let the gruff manner put him off. This was the first real chance he'd had to talk to him, and he wanted to find out what had frightened Prince in the woods and why the man had run away.

"I saw you playing with my dog Jake in the woods," he said chattily. "Do you like dogs?"

Another grunt.

"Jake really enjoyed—" Neil was beginning, when a shout from Brian Mason interrupted him. "Shut up at the back there, will you? We haven't got all day!"

Neil had to give up and start paying attention to the scene.

King Arthur and his knights rode in, with bright surcoats and shining armour. Brett Benson as Sir Lancelot carried a scarlet and gold banner. Neil and Emily and all the other villagers cheered, and Zeno came forward to offer their support to Arthur.

The run-through went perfectly, and Brian

decided to go for a take. The horsemen regrouped and rode into the village again, but when the time came for Max to talk to the king, Prince suddenly broke out into frantic barking, and tore off down the path towards the castle.

"Cut! Cut!" Brian yelled. "Somebody catch that dog!"

Max and Maggie Brown ran off together after Prince. Neil followed, fishing in his pocket under his costume for a dog treat to help coax the cocker spaniel back. By the time he caught up, Maggie already had a hand on Prince's collar, and Max was patting his dog to soothe him.

He looked up as Neil approached. "Something bothered him. He's not usually like this."

Neil squatted down and offered the titbit to Prince, who wolfed it down and looked for more. He had recovered from his shock, whatever it was, and trotted happily back towards the set at Max's heel.

Neil wondered whether to say something to Max about the extra. He didn't suppose that anyone else had noticed, but the man had been right next to Prince just before the dog took off. Prince had behaved just as he had in the wood the day before when they had met the man. It looked as if Prince didn't like him, but Neil didn't understand why.

The next take went well, but Brian Mason insisted on filming the scene a second time anyway. When he was satisfied, Neil and Emily went back to the castle to wash off their make-up and change into ordinary clothes. Then they headed for the kitchen to find Jake. The young Border collie threw himself at Neil to welcome him, leaping up with his tongue lolling out in a doggy grin.

"Hey, get down, you daft dog!" Neil rumpled Jake's ears. "I've been away two hours, not two months!"

The kitchen at Ainsworth Castle was a huge room, with oak beams holding up a white-washed ceiling. Copper pans hung on the walls, decorated with sprigs of holly from the greenery Neil and the others had collected the day before.

Along one side was an old-fashioned kitchen range, where Adrian Bartlett was making himself a cup of coffee. Princess was balancing on his shoe and trying to climb up his leg.

Adrian looked a bit harassed. "Is Max back?" he asked.

"No, he stayed to do another scene," said Neil. "Is Princess a problem?"

"I have to finish off the estate Christmas cards," Adrian explained. "And I shudder to think what she could get up to in the office! I daren't leave her, though, especially after what happened yesterday."

"I'll look after her," Emily said, scooping up Princess and cuddling the little pup close to her face. "Come on, gorgeous."

Adrian gave her a relieved smile. "Thanks, that's a big help." He took his coffee and went out, pausing in the doorway to say, "Penny's putting up decorations in the small drawing room, if you want to give her a hand."

The small drawing room was about the size of a tennis court. When Neil and Emily arrived, Penny was sorting shiny baubles from a large cardboard box. An enormous Christmas tree, without any decorations, stood in a tub on one side of the fireplace with a stepladder next to it. A bright fire was burning, and the room smelt of pine branches.

"Hello," Penny said, smiling. "I could do with some help. Better keep the dogs away, though. If they break these they could get hurt."

"Jake should be OK," Neil said, as the Border collie went to touch noses with King who was sprawled on the hearthrug. "Em, you'd better hang on to Princess."

Emily gave him a blissful smile. "No problem!"

Neil went up the ladder while Penny handed him the baubles.

"How did the filming go?" she asked.

"OK," said Neil. "But it was freezing cold down there. You're lucky your scenes are indoors!"

Penny laughed. "I have to do embroidery, though!" Pausing with a glittering ball in one hand, she added, "Was there any trouble?"

Emily was sitting cross-legged on the rug, while Princess scrambled all over her and covered her face with sloppy licks. She said, "Not really. We think that extra – the one Neil saw in the woods – might have spooked Prince a bit."

"I wonder who he is," said Neil. "Penny, do you know him?"

Penny shook her head. "Most of the extras are village people, but I've never seen him before."

Neil reached down for another bauble and fastened it carefully to a branch. "It's weird, because he helped Prince when the set collapsed, and he got on fine with Jake. I can't think why Prince has taken a dislike to him."

Penny shrugged. "Oh, well . . . That's not the big problem, though. What I want to know is who's trying to wreck the film. Verity told me what happened with the paint."

"Brett Benson was up there," Emily said. "And he was the one who found the paint spots on Prince."

Penny frowned and shook her head. "I can't believe it's him. Nobody's that stupid!" She fished in the box again. "Here's the star to go on top. Can you reach that far, Neil?"

Neil took the star and climbed up to stand precariously at the top of the ladder. While he leant over to fix the star to the topmost branch of the tree, he said, "I've been thinking. Whoever's doing this has to be able to come and go in the castle without anybody asking questions."

"That means the whole of the film crew," said Emily.

"And the people who live here," said Neil.

"But none of us would do it!" Penny protested. "We want the film to be made. The money's going to pay for all sorts of things."

Neil still wasn't used to the idea that a lord

who owned a castle could be short of money, but he knew that Penny was right. Lord Ainsworth really needed the fee from the production company.

"Yes, but . . . " An idea was nagging at Neil. A few things he'd ignored were starting to fit together. "You know, Adrian was up in the Long Gallery about the time the paint was spilt. He looked a bit funny, too, as if he didn't want to be seen up there."

"But Adrian's nice!" Emily protested. "And he was keen on the film from the start."

"I know." Neil tweaked the star into position

and climbed down to where he felt safer. "But that's not the only thing. He was supposed to be looking after Princess yesterday, when she got into trouble for chewing Jeff Calton's notes."

"He took Jake for a walk," said Emily.

"I just wonder if that's the only thing he did."

Penny had stopped unpacking the decorations and stood still, staring up at Neil. "That's . . . stupid," she said. "Why would Adrian try to spoil the film?"

"Not spoil it," said Neil. "Just delay it. You said yourself, your dad needs the money. And the longer the film crew are here, the more they'll have to pay to use the castle. I'm sorry, Penny. I'm really sorry. But Adrian—"

Penny had suddenly gone red with anger. "It's not Adrian – he wouldn't! I know he wouldn't! You are so arrogant, Neil Parker. You always think you're right, but really you don't know anything. I think you're horrible!"

She spun round and ran out of the door, slamming it behind her.

Chapter Seven

"Neil, you're an idiot," said Emily. The sound of the banging door drifted away. "How could you say all that in front of Penny?"

Neil came down the ladder. He felt awful. "I was just thinking aloud," he said. "I didn't want to upset her, but it's true, all the same. It could be Adrian. He's Lord Ainsworth's steward – it's his *job* to keep an eye on everything. He can go anywhere he likes in the castle and nobody would think twice about it. He might even think it's not really wrong, because the money would be to help Lord Ainsworth." He paused, and when Emily didn't say anything he challenged her. "Don't you think I'm right?"

Emily was still playing with Princess, running the little dog's silky ears through her fingers. "Maybe," she replied. "But it's hard to believe."

"I like Adrian as well," Neil said defensively. "But if he's innocent, why did he look so guilty this morning?"

Emily didn't answer. Neil put the lid back on the box of decorations; they couldn't carry on without Penny, and with so much bad stuff going on it was difficult to feel the proper excitement of Christmas. He remembered that in another two days they were supposed to be going home. He wasn't even sure that he would enjoy his own Christmas at King Street if he had to leave an unsolved mystery behind him. The quarrel with Penny made it even harder. Neil couldn't help thinking it was going to be the most miserable Christmas of his life.

The buffet lunch for the film crew was soup and sandwiches in the castle dining hall. Actors and crew were sitting on either side of the long dining table. Neil hoped to see Penny there because he wanted to apologize, but there was no sign of her. Making friends again would have to wait.

Max was there, drinking a mug of soup, with Prince sitting at his feet and looking up hopefully at the sandwich in his other hand. He grinned when he saw Neil and Emily.

"Hi. Things went really smoothly this morning. No problems at all."

"That's great." Neil fetched a plate of sandwiches to share with Emily, and they found themselves seats.

"I see you've got Princess," Max went on. "Thanks. Would you mind keeping her this afternoon? We're filming that scene again – the one where the inn collapsed."

"You'd better make sure it doesn't collapse again," Neil said, watching Emily give Princess a delighted hug.

"Jeff said he'd inspect it personally." Max drained his mug and put it down as Suzie, his chaperone, walked over, pointedly looking at her watch. "I'd better go. I'm due on set, and I have to visit make-up first."

He rushed off, followed by Prince. Neil fished a dog treat out of his pocket so that Jake wouldn't mind missing out on the sandwiches, and gave one to Emily for Princess.

"She's lovely!" said Emily. "Max is so lucky – apart from having to leave her and go off to film

192

all the time. Oh, and wear all that yucky make-up!" She stroked the pup's tiny head. "We'll have fun, though, won't we, girl?"

"Make-up!" said Neil. He'd just thought of something, and he couldn't believe it hadn't occurred to him before. "You're right, it's disgusting stuff. Nobody goes around in their make-up unless they're in a scene."

"So?" said Emily.

"So what was that guy – that weird extra – doing in make-up yesterday? They were repairing the village set and none of the peasants were needed. But he was in the make-up room first thing, and later on, when we saw him in the woods, he was *still* in costume."

Emily was tickling Princess's stomach. The little dog lay on her lap with her paws in the air, wriggling happily. "Maybe he likes being a peasant."

"Get real, Em! This could be important. Whoever's doing this doesn't want to be noticed. If you see somebody wandering around in costume, you just think he's something to do with the film."

Emily started to take him seriously. "You mean he isn't?"

"I don't know. But a peasant costume is a

good disguise, with all that gungy make-up. Maybe he's wearing it so that nobody will recognize him."

"But why?" Emily asked. "What does he get out of wrecking the film?"

"We won't know that until we know who he is."

Neil felt like kicking himself. He'd wasted time suspecting Brett Benson, and he'd even upset Penny by accusing Adrian, when all the time the most likely solution was staring him in the face.

"Prince doesn't like him, either," Emily said. "He runs away from him!"

Neil nodded. "He knows something's wrong, Em. I really wish he could talk!"

"Prince the dog detective!" Emily said, laughing. "Hey, Princess . . . don't kill my sweatshirt!" The tiny pup had seized her sleeve cuff and was tugging at it, growling fiercely. Emily gently took it away from her. Suddenly looking serious, she went on, "OK, Neil, suppose you're right. What are we going to do?"

Neil's first instinct was to tell Brian Mason, or Jeff Calton. But he'd got into enough trouble with Penny by not knowing when to keep quiet. This time he would have to be more careful.

"Whenever I've tried to talk to that extra, he's avoided me," he said. "This time I'm going to track him down. I'm going to find out who he is and what he thinks he's up to." He wolfed the last of his sandwich and stood up. "Are you coming?"

"Just try to stop me!" Emily replied, gathering up Princess in her arms. Jake followed them.

On their way to fetch their coats, they passed the old scullery which was being used as a make-up room. The door was open, and the same make-up girl was there, tidying away sticks of greasepaint.

Neil raised his eyebrows at Emily, who gave him the nod. "Hi," he said, going in. "Do you remember, yesterday – really early – you were making up one of the peasants? I wondered whether—"

"Now look," the girl interrupted. "I've told you before, I've got a job to do here. I don't want you in this room unless you're being made up. And I certainly haven't got time to answer stupid questions."

She turned away. Neil could still see her face in the mirror. It looked hot and angry.

He said, "Sor-*ree*," and left the room. "You

see?" he said to Emily. "There *is* something weird about that guy – and I bet she knows what it is!"

Muffled in coats and scarves, Neil and Emily trudged across the causeway and down the footpath towards the village set. Snow had started to fall again. Princess, tucked up in her favourite place inside Emily's jacket, licked at snowflakes that fell on her nose.

"This is what I reckon," said Neil. Jake followed him at ankle level. "We've got Princess, so he can't try anything with her, which means he's going to be hanging around where Prince is."

Instead of going straight down the path to the set, Neil steered them into the woods, working his way round towards the trailers on the far side. He thought they would have to hang around for ages, but as they emerged from behind the location catering van on the edge of the set, they almost collided with the extra going the other way.

Jake gave a welcoming bark, and bounced up to him. The extra ignored him, but Neil got his first really good look at the man's face. He couldn't help feeling that he should recognize him.

"Hello," he said. "I didn't know the peasants were filming today."

The extra turned away, muttering something.

"Just a minute," Neil said, wanting to delay him as he tried to remember where he had seen him before. The man ignored him, and started to walk away.

Emily said determinedly, "We wanted to ask you something. Are you—"

"Clear off. I'm busy," the man interrupted, an irritable expression on his face.

The bad-tempered look suddenly reminded Neil. He stood there gaping. When he spoke, he wasn't sure that his voice was going to come out right. "Harry Jenkins! That's who you are!"

The man ducked his head, and gave him a shifty look. "Don't know what you're talking about."

"Oh, yes, you do," Neil said. "I remember you now. You're Harry Jenkins. You were Prince's dog trainer when they filmed *The Time Travellers* at Padsham Castle."

Emily's eyes were like saucers. "Neil, you're right! I don't believe it!"

Neil went on. "Yes, you nearly wrecked that episode because you couldn't handle Prince.

Are you trying to wreck this one as well?"

Harry Jenkins didn't answer.

Neil was furious. Prince had taken the blame last time as well, until the truth had come out. "Does Jeff Calton know that you're on the set?" he asked. "I bet he doesn't. But he soon will."

"We'll see to that!" Emily added.

"Interfering kids," Harry Jenkins said. "It was your fault I had to leave my job last time." He prodded Neil in the chest. "I haven't worked since. Everybody knows what happened, and nobody will give me a job as a dog trainer now. So I signed on as an extra. So what?"

Neil almost felt sorry for him. Last time he'd lost his nerve because a dog had bitten him, and that wasn't his fault. But he had been wrong to try to carry on with his job and then blame his problems on Prince. And Neil was beginning to feel certain that Harry Jenkins was to blame for all the recent disasters.

"That's not all, is it?" he asked. "You're not just an extra. Is it you who's been causing all the trouble? Just so you can get back at Prince for what happened. Did you mess with the stairs on the set, so the whole thing fell apart? Did you put Princess where she could chew Mr Mason's notes, and—"

"I don't know what you're talking about," Harry Jenkins interrupted.

"I think you do."

"No wonder Prince doesn't like you," Emily said. "He knew who you were all along!"

"It's got nothing to do with me," Jenkins insisted. "I just needed the job. And if you go round saying it's my fault, you'll find yourselves in trouble. So keep your mouths shut!"

He shoved Neil to one side and stormed off through the trees.

The man's stern words didn't frighten Neil. He stood watching Jenkins until he was out of sight, and then whistled for Jake, who had run a few paces after him and now stood looking back as if he didn't understand what was going on.

"We've got to tell somebody," said Emily,

gently soothing Princess who was still tucked down her front.

"Right," said Neil. "Brian Mason's on set, so let's go and look for Jeff Calton. We've got to make him see that none of these accidents are the dogs' fault."

When they got back to Ainsworth Castle, Jeff Calton was standing at the end of the causeway, talking to a couple of people in a car. They were in uniform; Neil thought they must be the security staff Jeff had sent for.

He gave Emily a glance and went up to speak to him. "Mr Calton—"

Jeff Calton didn't look at him. "Not now, Neil."

"But this is important."

"I said, not now. I have to brief these people."

"But—"

Ignoring him, Jeff got into the car and said to the driver, "Straight ahead. I'll show you where to park."

The car swept off, across the causeway and under the arch into the castle courtyard.

"Well!" said Emily indignantly.

Neil stared after the car in frustration. He'd solved the mystery of why so much was going wrong with the film, and now the producer wouldn't listen to him. How long would it be before Harry Jenkins thought of something else to do?

Then he heard a voice calling his name. He turned to see Max and Prince making their way up from the village. "It went great!" Max said, smiling. "Brian was really pleased." He tickled Princess on her nose. "Hi there, midget! Have you missed your dad?" Then his smile vanished as he saw the expression on Neil's face. "Is something the matter?"

"You bet. Listen to this."

As they walked towards the castle, and Neil talked, he could see that Max was getting just as furious as he was feeling himself. "Harry Jenkins!" he said. "He nearly got Prince dropped from the show! And this time it's worse – Prince could have been hurt."

He squatted down in the courtyard and hugged Prince. Prince, not understanding, put his paws up on Max's knee and slurped his tongue across his face.

Max laughed. "Oh, Prince, you're great!" Then he looked up at Neil, his laughter vanishing. "What do you think we should do?"

"We've got to make somebody listen," Emily

said indignantly. "We've got to get rid of that man somehow."

"Where's Brian Mason?" Neil asked.

"Still on set. He's filming a scene with Morgan and the Black Knight."

"Then we'll tell him when he's finished. He'll have to do something. And while we're waiting . . . " he paused, "let's give the dogs a good run!"

Neil hung around in the castle courtyard while Max changed out of his costume. Emily had gone to find Penny, to tell her everything and make up the quarrel. Neil was sorry he had ever suspected Adrian, and he hoped that Adrian himself would never find out. All the same, he still wanted to know why the steward had been so hot and bothered that morning in the Long Gallery.

Jake gave a welcoming bark as Max and Prince hurried down the steps from the main castle entrance. Max was carrying Princess, but he put her down once he was in the courtyard. She sniffed at the slush and tried to shake it off her paws, and then skidded after Jake and Prince as they headed out under the archway.

"That's better," said Neil. "They haven't had a good run all day."

He was beginning to get over his anger as he followed the dogs across the causeway and took the footpath that led alongside the lake. It was good to get out with Jake and forget about the problems of the filming.

Max felt the same, Neil was sure. After a few minutes he found a stick for the dogs to chase. Both Prince and Jake bounded after it, barking madly and sending up flurries of snow. Princess scampered along after them, adding her high-pitched yapping, her floppy ears flying up and down.

Max laughed as Prince brought the stick back to him, feathery tail wagging. "Good boy! Let Jake have a go this time. Go, Jake – fetch!"

"Oh, no!" Neil exclaimed. "Look at Princess!"

The little pup had given up the race for the stick. Someone had built a snowman by the lake, and Princess hurled herself at it with shrill barks of delight, tugging at the brightly coloured scarf around its neck. As she pulled, the head of the snowman rolled off and plumped down into the snow, half burying the tiny dog.

"Hey, she'll hurt herself!" Max said, running towards her.

"No, she's fine!" Neil ached from laughing as he watched Princess scrabble out of the snowdrift with the scarf draped around her neck.

Max scooped her up and took the scarf off. "Terror! Look what you've done."

He put her down and she scurried off again, dancing around in circles as if she was trying to catch her own tail, before dashing off to join her dad and Jake who were hunting around the roots of some bushes near the lake shore.

The lake was still covered with ice, and on the surface there were marks where people had been sliding and skating.

Neil was just going to suggest to Max that they should be getting back when the three dogs broke away from the bushes and ran out onto the ice. Prince was in the lead, with Jake close behind and Princess scampering along at the rear.

"Jake! Hey, Jake!" Neil yelled. Once again he could see in his mind the ice cracking to swallow up his dog in the dark water. "Jake, come here!"

Jake didn't come. Max shouted for Prince. The cocker spaniel stopped and then came trotting back, but Jake and Princess stayed out on the ice, gambolling around each other and gradually moving further and further away from the shore.

As Prince came panting up, Max took out his lead and clipped it on. Neil was psyching himself up to go out there and fetch Jake when Max thrust the loop of Prince's lead into his hand.

"I'll get them," he said.

Neil managed a weak smile. "Thanks."

He stood watching with Prince beside him as Max walked out onto the ice. Max kept calling the dogs, and eventually they both ran towards him. Neil saw him bend over to pick up Princess. Then, as he straightened up again he seemed to stagger, and yelled something Neil couldn't catch. Jake started to bark. As Neil stared, transfixed, he saw a dark line open up in the ice, and Max went plunging down into the waters of the lake.

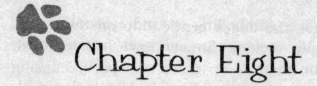

Chapter Eight

For a few seconds Neil was panic-stricken. All his instincts told him to dash back to the castle, yelling for help. But then he came to his senses – help from the castle might be too late for Max and the dogs. Neil knew he had to do something now.

He stooped and unclipped Prince's lead. "Prince, go! Tell them at the castle!"

Prince looked up at him, whining softly, his intelligent eyes puzzled. Neil felt frustrated, not knowing exactly what commands Max used for Prince.

"Find Maggie," he said. "Go and fetch help! Go, Prince, go!"

He turned Prince's head towards the castle

and gave the dog a gentle slap on the rump. Somehow Prince must have understood, because he took off down the path, barking furiously as he ran.

Neil turned back to the lake. In spite of the gathering twilight, he could still see Max's head and shoulders, and a smaller black shape that he thought must be Jake. There was no sign of Princess at all.

His throat was dry. He told himself that he would only make things worse if he went out there to help. But he knew he could not just stand there and watch Max and the dogs drown because he was too scared to do anything.

A faint cry came across the ice from Max. "Help! Neil, get help!"

Desperately, Neil tugged a dead branch free of the undergrowth. Then, swallowing his fear, he crawled out onto the frozen lake on hands and knees so as not to put too much pressure on the fragile ice, pushing the branch in front of him.

He could see dark water slopping under the skin of ice. A few metres out from the shore he thought he could hear the ice start to creak, and feeling it shifting under him he lay flat and edged forward slowly on his stomach.

As he drew closer, he could see Max trying to grab the edge of the ice with one hand, but it kept breaking away. With his other hand he was clutching Princess. The little dog was limp, not moving.

Max was treading water, trying to keep afloat, but Neil could see that he was already exhausted. His hair was soaking wet, as if his head had gone under at least once.

Close beside Max, Jake was standing on an ice floe which had broken away from the rest. It floated, but water was washing over it. Jake's paws were splayed out as he fought for balance, and he was whining miserably.

"Max!" Neil yelled. "Here!"

Max saw him there for the first time. "Neil!" he gasped. "Keep back – it's all breaking up."

"Grab this." Neil pushed the branch out as far as he could so that Max could hang on to it and pull himself up to the edge of the ice. "Give me Princess!"

With something to grasp, Max managed to drag himself a little way out of the water and pass the pup across to Neil.

Princess looked unbelievably tiny, with her coat plastered to her body. Her head lolled as Neil took her, and she didn't move.

"She's dead!" Max sobbed. "I know she's dead!"

"No she's not," said Neil, though he couldn't tell.

Sprawled out on the ice, he couldn't do anything to help Princess or to get her warm. He yelled to Jake, but the collie couldn't get across to the main sheet of ice, and Neil couldn't reach him. He made one effort to grab Max's shoulders and haul him out, but when he tried, more of the surface near him cracked and water surged over it, soaking him through. The ice felt increasingly unsteady under him. He knew he couldn't go back now. All he could do was hang on.

"Prince went for help," he said to Max. "It won't be long."

He tried not to show how scared he was, for himself and Max, and especially for the dogs. Princess needed help quickly; even if she was still alive, she wouldn't survive the cold for much longer.

Then, to his relief, Neil heard movement and voices from the lakeside. Someone shouted, "Don't move, Neil. We're coming!" and Neil tried to look over his shoulder, but his movement made the ice tilt alarmingly.

From then on, he kept as still as he could for what seemed like an age. Then, he heard a voice much closer behind him. "Neil, move backwards. There's a ladder here."

It was Adrian Bartlett. Neil felt almost too scared to move, but he edged back and felt hands guiding him until his feet made contact with the top rung of a ladder. He moved backwards until he was lying on it. Now he risked another glance over his shoulder and saw that a system of ladders and planks had been laid out for support across the ice.

Adrian moved forward on another ladder. He gripped Max under the arms, helping him through the splintering ice to the end of the ladder.

"Adrian!" Neil called. "What about Jake?"

"I'll get Jake." Adrian didn't turn to look at him. "Go back to shore."

There was nothing Neil could do except obey.

Clutching Princess to him, he managed to crawl backwards until he reached the firmer ice at the edge of the lake. Lord Ainsworth, Maggie Brown and Emily were waiting to help him back onto the shore.

"Maggie!" he gasped, shaking from cold as he held out the little pup's limp body. "Look . . . we've got to do something."

Maggie took Princess in firm, capable hands.

"Is she dead?" Emily asked, agonized.

Maggie pinched Princess's toes, and to Neil's delight he saw her eyelids twitch. A grin spread over Maggie's face. "No, she's not dead."

Quickly Maggie checked Princess's heartbeat, then held her upside down by her back legs. Neil almost protested when he saw her dangling like that, until he realized that water was trickling out of her mouth.

Then Maggie laid Princess on her side, and opened her mouth to pull her tongue forward and make sure nothing was blocking her airway. "Got to get her breathing," she muttered.

Holding Princess's muzzle to keep her mouth closed, Maggie placed her own mouth around Princess's nose, and blew. Princess's chest rose and fell. Maggie took a breath and said, "Neil, check her heartbeat."

Neil laid his hand against Princess's side and nodded as he felt the faint fluttering. Maggie blew into her nostrils again. Again. And again.

"Princess!" Max appeared and collapsed to his knees beside the pup. He was soaked through and shivering convulsively, but he never took his eyes off her.

Neil kept his hand in place to monitor the heartbeat, and gave a cry of relief as he felt it strengthen and the rise and fall of Princess's chest become automatic as the little pup started breathing again.

He realized for the first time that Emily was crouched beside him, clutching painfully at his arm. She had tears on her face. "Will she be all right?" she asked Maggie.

"She'll be fine," Maggie promised. "But she needs warming up right now. I'll take her."

Carrying Princess, she set off to the castle at a run. Neil turned back to the lake. Relief flooded over him as he saw Adrian pulling Jake back onto dry land. When the steward carried him over, Neil thanked him and then squatted down beside the Border collie to put his arms round him.

"Jake, you dimbo!" he said, but his voice was shaking and he had to make an effort not to cry.

He couldn't face the thought of losing Jake as well as Sam. "Don't you dare do that again!"

When he was sure that Jake had come to no real harm, Neil also headed for the castle, the Border collie running alongside him. He and Max caught up with Maggie in the small drawing room. She was towelling Princess gently in front of the fire. Princess's eyes were still closed, but she was breathing normally and her coat was already dry.

King and Fred were both sitting beside the fire, looking down at Princess almost as if they were guarding her.

Neil took one of the towels and rubbed Jake

dry. The young Border collie seemed quieter than usual, but Neil didn't think there was much wrong with him. He'd been lucky to have escaped the worst of the freezing water.

Max stooped over Princess and stroked her. "Thanks, Maggie," he said unsteadily. "And you, Neil. I really thought she was dead."

"The vet's on his way," said Maggie. "But you're really not helping, standing there dripping over her. Go and get into some dry clothes."

Max struggled to smile, but he was still shivering and his teeth were chattering with cold. Neil grabbed him and propelled him out of the room. "Come on. Or they'll be holding up the filming for *you* this time."

When Neil and Max had changed, they went back to the drawing room where Penny was serving out hot drinks to the rescuers. Neil wrapped his hands round a mug of hot chocolate and took a gulp; the scalding liquid brought tears to his eyes.

"Thanks," he said. "Er . . . Penny, I'm really sorry about what I said before. I know now it wasn't Adrian."

Penny gave him a hard look, and then she

smiled. "I know – Emily told me. It's OK, Neil. It did look a bit odd." She glanced across the room to where Adrian was slumped in an armchair near the fire. "Now, go and thank him for pulling you out of the lake."

A wave of embarrassment flooded over Neil, almost as if Adrian knew what suspicions he'd had. "Yes, I will . . . " he said.

He was relieved to be able to put it off for a while, because he'd noticed the local vet, David Blackburn, bending over Princess by the fire. He was a fair-haired young man with big, gentle hands. Max was with him, and Neil went over to hear what the vet was saying.

"She'll sleep for a while now, and the best thing you can do is leave her to it. Keep her quiet for a day or two. And if there are any problems, phone me right away. I'll be at home over the Christmas break."

He ran a hand over Princess's coat. The little spaniel stirred, opened her soft brown eyes to look at Max, and settled down again.

"She will be OK, won't she?" Max asked anxiously.

David smiled. "She'll be fine."

While the vet was busy giving Jake a check-up, Max's chaperone Suzie came in. "Max, the doctor's here to check you over."

Max looked up from Princess. "I'm OK, really."

"You're OK when the doctor says you are. You too, Neil. Or what will I tell your mum and dad?"

Neil and Max looked at each other and shrugged.

"All right." Max got up and went to the door, and then stopped. "Just a minute," he said. "Where's Prince?"

Neil gazed around him as if he expected Prince to pop out from behind the nearest piece of furniture. In all the confusion, and the worry about Princess, he hadn't realized that the cocker spaniel wasn't around.

"I sent him up here for help," he said. "Somebody must have seen him."

"I was in the estate office when I heard him barking," Adrian said.

"But where did Prince go after that?" Max asked.

Maggie Brown remembered following Prince down to the lake with the other rescuers. Nobody had seen him since.

"He wasn't at the lake when I arrived," Adrian said. "I kept an eye open for him because I was afraid he would go out on the ice."

"He must be around here somewhere," Lord Ainsworth said. "We'd better look."

Efficiently he divided everybody up into search teams to cover all of the castle. Suzie hauled Max off to the doctor, but Neil managed to slip away to join Penny and Emily who were assigned to the Long Gallery and the rooms just off it. Though they searched everywhere carefully they found no clues, and Prince did not answer when they called.

Suddenly, Neil noticed that there was a folded sheet of paper lying on the Round Table in the Great Hall.

"What's that?" he asked.

Emily shrugged. "More production notes?"

Neil went over and picked up the paper, unfolded it, and stood staring. "Come and look at this!"

The others crowded round. The paper carried a message, written in black capital letters. It read:

I WANT £5000. PUT IT IN THE HOLLOW TREE
AT THE TOP OF THE LANE BY TOMORROW NIGHT.
DON'T TELL THE POLICE, OR YOU WON'T SEE
PRINCE AGAIN.

Chapter Nine

All the other searchers had returned to the drawing room when Neil and the others went back with the ransom note. Max was there, too, with Princess sleeping on his lap, bundled up in a blanket; the tiny pup was twitching in her sleep. Max stroked her head. His mouth was tight, as if he was trying to hold in his worry.

"Look at this," said Neil. As they read the note, passing it from hand to hand, Neil explained what he suspected about Harry Jenkins.

"Jenkins!" Jeff Calton exclaimed. "I'd no idea . . . I never even noticed that he was on set."

"That's because he was always in costume

and make-up," Neil said. "He didn't want to risk being recognized. He must be out to wreck the film because he thinks it was Prince's fault that he lost his job as a dog trainer."

"That's rubbish," Jeff said. "He lost his job because he couldn't cope and then tried to lie about it."

"So what do we do now?" Maggie asked.

Max had gone white. "I'll have to pay it. Or he'll kill Prince."

"But have you got five thousand pounds?" Penny asked. "It's an awful lot of money."

"I'm not sure . . . I think so. At least – what I earn from *The Time Travellers* goes into a fund for me, for later. There must be a way to get at it. I'm going to phone Dad."

He got up, gently set Princess down on the rug in front of the fire beside King and Fred, and went out.

Neil read the note again, as if it could tell him something else. As well as being anxious about Prince, he was starting to feel guilty. If he hadn't confronted Harry Jenkins, maybe he would have just gone on trying to find ways to disrupt the filming. That had been bad enough, but nothing like the disaster they were faced with now. Neil was afraid that he'd pushed

Jenkins into one last effort to get revenge on the dog he thought had ruined his career.

And unless they could come up with an idea quickly, he was going to get away with it.

"We've got to get Prince back," Jeff Calton said, rubbing his hands through his hair until it stuck up in a crest. "We can't carry on filming until we do. I'll have a word with our security people."

"I'd call the police," said Lord Ainsworth. "They'll soon find—"

"No." The interruption came from Max, who had reappeared in the doorway. He looked tense and his voice was shaking. "If you do, he'll kill Prince. He says so."

He came into the room, sat on the hearthrug beside Princess, and started to stroke the sleeping pup's silky head. "I talked to Mum," he said. "She and Dad will come down tomorrow, and see what they can do about the money."

Emily went to sit beside him. "We'll get Prince back," she said. "He'll be OK."

"Sure he will," said Jeff.

"Listen, Max," said Neil. "I don't think Harry Jenkins wants to hurt Prince. Remember, he helped to get him out when the village inn collapsed. He must have loved dogs once, or he wouldn't have been a trainer."

"He even played with Jake in the woods," Emily added.

Max said nothing, still intent on stroking Princess. Neil felt helpless. He didn't know what else they could do.

Beside the fire stood the Christmas tree; somebody had finished decorating it, and the glass ornaments and tinsel glittered in the firelight. Neil could hardly believe it would be Christmas in a couple of days. He had too much on his mind to look forward to it properly.

The silence was broken by Jeff Calton. "I'd better tell Brian. He's not going to like this."

"He's not to call the police," Max said sharply.

"No, don't worry," Adrian said. "Nobody will do anything without talking to you first. Anyway, we could do without this kind of publicity."

When Jeff had gone, Neil flung himself into a chair and scratched Jake's ears as his dog padded up beside him. "I hate letting Harry Jenkins get away with it," he said. "It really bugs me, just thinking that he's got Prince somewhere—" He broke off. "Hey, that's it! Where *is* he keeping Prince?"

221

"Is he staying in the castle?" Emily asked.

Penny stared at her. "No, the extras aren't—" She stopped suddenly, as if she had just understood.

Adrian started to pace the room. "The principal actors and the film crew are all staying in the West Wing. We took on some more staff to look after them. The extras are local people, so they live at home and come in for the filming."

"Jenkins isn't a local," Maggie said. "So where is he staying?"

Neil sat up in his seat. "He must be somewhere close, so he can pick up the ransom. And it must be somewhere he could hide Prince . . ."

Max glanced up from stroking Princess, suddenly starting to look hopeful. "You really think we could find him?"

"What about a hotel?" Maggie asked.

"There's only the Ainsworth Arms in Beckthwaite," said Adrian.

Lord Ainsworth shook his head. "He wouldn't risk being seen with Prince."

"So where is he?" Penny asked.

"Just a minute," said Neil. "What about that weird make-up girl? She knows something about Jenkins, I bet she does!"

"What make-up girl?" asked Maggie.

"We don't know her name," Emily explained. "But she was doing Jenkins's make-up when he wasn't supposed to be on set, and when we asked her about him she was really nasty!"

"Is she staying here?" asked Penny.

"She should be," said Adrian.

"There's one of the make-up assistants, called Shirley, in the room next to mine," said Maggie. "She's been very snappy ever since we arrived."

Neil sprang to his feet. "What are we waiting for?"

But when Maggie took them to Shirley's room, Shirley wasn't there, and when they asked some of the other make-up girls no one knew where she was. Their only link to Harry Jenkins had disappeared.

"We're going home tomorrow," Emily said gloomily, winding her scarf round her neck.

"No, we're not," said Neil, as he clipped Jake's lead onto his collar. "I'm not going anywhere until Max has Prince back."

As Neil got ready to walk Jake the following morning, he felt depressed. His brilliant idea had fizzled out. This morning Shirley hadn't turned up for work. That was enough to make Neil certain she was involved with Harry Jenkins, but it didn't help in tracking either of them down.

The trail to Prince had gone cold, and without him filming had come to a complete stop.

"But tomorrow's Christmas Eve," Emily pointed out. "We can't stay here for Christmas unless we're invited. Besides, Mum and Dad will go spare!"

"I don't care," Neil said determinedly. "I'm not leaving Max. Anyway, could you manage to enjoy Christmas knowing Prince isn't safe?"

Emily shook her head. "I don't think anybody's going to enjoy Christmas!"

Neil pushed open the heavy oak door and looked out. Thick icicles hung from the lintel; the steps and the courtyard were covered by a fresh fall of snow. At his feet, Jake whined uneasily, and tugged against the lead.

"Oh, no," Neil said. Even though he thought he'd overcome his own fear of water, he wasn't going to risk Jake on the ice again. "You're not running free today, boy. You're not going anywhere near that lake!"

He and Emily were venturing out into the snow when Max came along the passage, with

Princess on a lead. Neil was glad to see that the little pup was trotting along beside him, looking as perky as if the day before had been a dream.

"Hello, there!" Emily said, crouching down to fondle the dog's long ears. "How is she, Max?"

"She seems fine. She's been whimpering a bit, though. I think she misses Prince, and can't understand why he's not here."

Emily ruffled the pup's golden fur. "We'll find your dad, Princess, I promise!"

"What about the filming?" Neil asked.

Max shrugged. "Brian's talking about getting a stand-in for Prince, so we can carry on. But it won't be the same. I don't want to work with another dog."

Neil clapped him on the shoulder. "It's tough."

Max shrugged again. "Are you going out?" he asked. "I'll come with you. Maggie said it would be OK to take Princess out for a bit."

Before he had finished pulling on his thick jacket and boots, they were joined by Penny, with both King and Fred beside her.

"I feel like harnessing these two to the sledge," she said, laughing.

Neil couldn't help grinning, even though he was worried. "With a sack and a Father

Christmas outfit! That'd be really worth seeing!"

Penny put both the huge dogs on their leads, and handed Fred's to Emily. They were heading out towards the lake shore, when Princess suddenly tugged on the lead and started whining.

"Maybe she's scared to go down there," Emily suggested.

"It's OK," Max said, stooping to pick up the little dog. Princess evaded his hands, and started snuffling at something by the side of the path.

"Hang on a minute," Neil said. "Let's see what she does."

The spaniel pup kept her nose down for a minute, and then pulled on the lead in the direction of the medieval village. Neil and Max looked at each other.

"Do you think she knows something?" Max asked, as if he could hardly dare believe it.

"She can't be tracking Prince," said Emily. "She's too little."

"Cocker spaniels have really good scenting skills," Neil said. "I reckon we should follow her."

They started to move down the path to the village, with Princess scuttling along in the

lead, tail waving wildly. Then as they approached the set she hesitated, trotted back to Max and away again to sniff at Jake.

"She's lost it," Max said, disappointed.

"Maybe, but I haven't," said Neil. "I've just remembered something . . . I think I know where Harry Jenkins is!"

"Where?" Max's voice was sharp with anxiety. "What do you mean?"

"The trailers by the medieval village." Neil pointed down the path to where the trailers were just in sight. "Look, Princess has brought us nearly there. One of them is being used for make-up on the set. I bet Shirley's letting Harry stay in it!"

"We saw him in the woods that day," Emily added. "He could have been on his way there."

"And he was lurking round there when we met him yesterday," said Neil. "It's worth a try. Come on!"

Chapter Ten

They set off at a run towards the medieval village, the dogs bounding alongside. No one was on set this morning, and the trailers looked quiet and deserted. As they paused on the edge of the village, Princess started barking, and danced around on the end of her lead.

"She knows her dad's here!" said Emily.

"Now what do we do?" asked Penny.

"I'm going to see who's in there," Neil said.

"No, wait . . ." Max sounded panicky, but Neil was already marching out into the clearing and across to the make-up trailer.

He rapped on the door. There was a moment's silence, then a scuffling noise from inside, and the door opened a crack. Shirley, the make-up girl, peered out.

Neil hadn't thought what to say, but now that he was faced with her, his mind worked fast. "Hello," he said. "I've got a message for Harry Jenkins. He is here, isn't he?"

Shirley looked terrified. She said, "I don't know what you're talking about!" and shut the door firmly.

Neil stepped back and scanned the trailer. He was sure that Jenkins and Prince were there, but he couldn't see anything through the blinds that covered the windows. Slowly, he walked back to his friends.

"We've got to get in there somehow," said Penny.

"But if we try anything, he'll kill Prince," Max protested.

"No, I don't think he will," said Neil. "I don't think he would hurt a dog, whatever he says. If we—"

Princess interrupted him. She was still tugging at her lead, and now she burst out into another flurry of excited barking.

"Good girl!" said Neil. "You can smell your dad, can't you?"

Before he had finished speaking, an

answering bark came from the trailer.

"Prince!" Max exclaimed. "That's Prince!"

"All right!" said Neil.

"Listen, Max." Penny was speaking quickly. "We've got to tell the police now. We know he's got a stolen dog in there. I know the sergeant at Beckthwaite. He won't do anything stupid. I'm going to phone."

Taking King with her, she headed back towards the castle. Max watched her go, and then stooped to pick up Princess, who was still barking furiously. He hugged her to him. "It'll be OK," he promised. Neil thought he was trying to convince himself.

He took a few steps out into the clearing. Raising his voice, he called, "Mr Jenkins! We know you're in there. Bring Prince out now and you'll save yourself a lot of trouble."

Emily whispered behind him, "Don't mention the police." Neil nodded. There was no answer from the trailer except for more barking from Prince. The noise set Jake off as well, and Fred added a deep woof too.

Neil had to calm Jake down before he could make himself heard again. "Mr Jenkins! Let Prince come out. You're only—"

The door of the trailer opened. Harry Jenkins

appeared, with Prince on a lead.

"Prince!" Max called. "Here, Prince!"

Prince pulled towards him to the full length of his lead, barking louder than ever. Harry Jenkins hesitated, as if he might decide to hand the cocker spaniel over, and then wrenched on the lead and dragged Prince away. Prince was still barking, trying to resist and go to Max, skidding and slithering through the snow as Jenkins jerked on the lead.

Neil took off in pursuit. Harry Jenkins was floundering up the slope which led to the road, stumbling in unseen hollows and slipping backwards as the snow gave way under his feet. Prince, still hanging back, managed to get his lead caught up in a bramble bush. As Jenkins stopped to unwind it, Neil hurled himself at him and grabbed him round the waist. Jenkins fell backwards with Neil on top of him.

Prince tugged himself free, and dashed off in a flurry of snow, back down the slope towards Max.

As he struggled to hang on to Harry Jenkins, Neil could hear wild barking from the dogs as the others forced their way through the snowy undergrowth. Jenkins threw Neil off, but before he could get to his feet Emily had caught up and grabbed him, and Neil heard another voice shouting his name from lower down the hill.

He got a grip on Harry, and looked back to see Lord Ainsworth, Penny and Maggie Brown hurrying towards them through the trees. At the bottom of the slope, Max was kneeling in the snow with Prince in his arms. Princess danced around them madly, yapping at the top of her tiny voice.

Harry fought to stand upright, but with both Neil and Emily hanging on to him, and Fred and Jake both standing by, he couldn't run. Panting, he faced Lord Ainsworth. "Get them off me!"

"I think they're doing a splendid job." Lord Ainsworth's voice was cold. "Maybe you'd like to explain what you're doing with a stolen dog?"

Harry Jenkins opened his mouth, but nothing came out. He sagged in Neil's grasp.

Neil called to Max, "Is he hurt, Max?"

Max was looking Prince over carefully. "No, I think he's fine."

"I wouldn't have hurt him," Jenkins protested. "I'd have given him back."

Lord Ainsworth snorted disbelievingly. "Maybe. In any case, you can explain all that to the police."

As he spoke, there was the sound of a car engine, and a police car slowly nosed its way down the track that led to the clearing, and parked beside the trailer. A police sergeant got out of it. Lord Ainsworth grabbed Harry's shoulder and propelled him back towards the car.

Neil and Emily followed. Beside the trailer, the make-up girl was sitting on a fallen log, crying quietly.

"Shirley, what are you doing mixed up in all this?" Maggie asked her.

Shirley looked up at her. "He's my brother," she said. "I didn't want anything to do with it. And I didn't know he was going to steal the dog."

"That's right, she didn't," Jenkins said. "She let me sleep in the make-up van and made me up – but that's all."

"I'm sorry, miss," the police sergeant said. "You'll have to come with us and make a statement."

Shirley got up, wiping her face with a handkerchief. "It's all gone wrong," she said. "And now I'll lose my job as well."

"I'll talk to Jeff," Maggie promised, but as Shirley got into the police car she didn't look as if she thought that would do much good.

Harry Jenkins glanced back to where Max was still crouching beside Prince. Princess was touching noses with her dad. Harry opened his mouth to say something but as Max caught his eye he looked away and got into the car in silence. The sergeant drove off. Neil watched the car edge its way back up the track, wheels spinning to get a grip on the snow as it vanished among the trees.

"Let's hope that's the last of him," he said with satisfaction.

"Yes," said Penny, "and now we can get on with the film."

"There's only one problem," said Maggie. "Tomorrow's Christmas Eve. Jeff told me this

235

morning that we can't possibly finish filming before Christmas. If we have to strike the sets and then come back afterwards, it's going to cost the earth."

"You mean the film might still be ruined?" Max asked, dismayed.

Neil and Emily looked at each other. They couldn't believe that after all their efforts Harry Jenkins might have done what he set out to do.

"Just a minute," said Lord Ainsworth. "What's all this about striking the sets? Is there any reason why you can't stay here and finish?"

"But it's Christmas," said Maggie. "You can't want the castle full of film people over Christmas."

Lord Ainsworth's face, reddened from the cold, broke into a beaming smile. "Why not?"

Maggie gaped at him. "Why not . . . well . . . "

"You'll all be very welcome. Max, your parents are on their way already – they'll be welcome to stay too. We'll all have a real medieval Christmas in Ainsworth Castle!"

Neil thought it was a great idea. The only problem was, he and Emily were due to go home. He was trying not to feel too disappointed when Penny came and grabbed his arm.

"Dad, we can invite Neil and Emily's mum

and dad, can't we? And their little sister?"

"What?" Lord Ainsworth peered down at Neil and Emily. "Yes, of course we can. Let them all come!"

Lord Ainsworth got to his feet and rapped the table for silence. As he waited, Neil looked around the Great Hall of Ainsworth Castle. Snow was swirling past the windows, but inside logs blazed up in the enormous fireplace. Bright lights shone on the Arthurian weapons and tapestries, and on the tables set for a magnificent Christmas dinner.

Penny had suggested using the Round Table for the Christmas feast, but the props master had refused to risk damaging it, so long tables had been set up in a huge square, with white linen cloths and red candles in holders made from holly and pine cones. Silver cutlery and crystal glasses sparkled at each place setting.

Verity the wardrobe mistress had surpassed herself to find costumes for everyone. Neil wore a blue velvet tunic instead of his peasant outfit, and both Emily and Penny wore long dresses. Penny's brother Rick, just home from music college, was dressed as a medieval minstrel. Even the guests were in costume. Neil thought Carole, his mum, really suited her long, trailing gown of red velvet, though Bob Parker, his dad, looked a bit uncomfortable in a knight's heavy robes. Five-year-old Sarah, dressed as one of Morgan le Fay's imps, had hardly been able to stop twirling around to admire herself, and was wriggling excitedly in her chair.

It wasn't often that Bob and Carole left King Street Kennels, but Carole had told Neil that with help from Kate and Bev, the kennel maids, they'd arranged to stay at the castle overnight and go home the next day.

King and Fred were sprawled in front of the fire, just like the hounds in a real medieval hall, but Jake sat beside Neil's chair, and Prince beside Max. Neil wasn't sure where Princess had got to. He'd been about to ask Max when Lord Ainsworth called for silence.

Gradually everyone was quietening down. Neil grinned across the table at Max and his parents, Fred's owner Bill Grey, and the rest of the actors and film crew who were sitting nearby. Everyone looked happy except Brett Benson. Maggie had told Neil that he was sulking because he'd planned to jet off to the Bahamas for Christmas and had to cancel it because of the filming. *Serves him right*, Neil thought.

The only member of the film crew who wasn't there was Shirley. Jeff Calton had pulled her off the film, but Maggie had persuaded him not to sack her. She had gone home for Christmas with her brother Harry who was out on bail until his case came up for trial. No one knew what his sentence would be, but one thing was certain: his career with dogs was finished. Neil thought there couldn't be a worse punishment.

"Before we start to eat," Lord Ainsworth

began, "I'd like to say a few words. First, to welcome all of you to Ainsworth Castle. It must be hundreds of years since a Lord Ainsworth sat down to eat with such splendid company."

So let's get on with it, Neil pleaded silently. *I'm starving!*

"I'd also like to wish you a very happy Christmas, and to our friends from Prince Productions a successful conclusion to their filming. I'm sure we're all glad to hear that Prince is safe and well, and I for one am looking forward to seeing Ainsworth Castle on the screen as Camelot."

Scratching his moustache and smiling a little, he went on, "One of you film people told me that it was King Arthur's custom never to sit down to a feast before he'd heard a piece of wonderful news. I think we ought to stick to these old customs, and so I've got some news I'd like to share with you. Adrian . . . ?"

"What's all this about?" Neil asked Emily.

Emily just shrugged, but Penny's eyes were sparkling, as if she knew something they didn't.

Adrian had gone scarlet, and looked embarrassed as he got to his feet and cleared his throat. "Er . . . yes . . . well, I'm delighted to announce that Verity, who some of you know is wardrobe mistress for Prince Productions, and as you can all see is doing a marvellous job . . ." He paused, and gave up the tangled sentence. "I asked Verity to marry me, and she said yes."

Applause broke out all round the table. Verity looked pink and smiled.

Neil nearly choked into his drink. "That's why he was lurking up in the Long Gallery!"

"And why he looked so hot and bothered," said Emily. "I bet Brett Benson caught him chatting up Verity!"

Lord Ainsworth took over again. "So Verity will be leaving Prince Productions, but she's going to set up a display of costumes here at Ainsworth Castle, for the visitors who come to see where the film was made. And I'm sure we all hope that she and Adrian will be very happy. Will you all drink a toast, please, to Adrian and Verity."

Everyone rose to their feet and raised their glasses. "Adrian and Verity!"

Waiters came in from one end of the hall with roast turkeys on huge silver platters, dishes of vegetables, sauces and gravy boats. Neil didn't know if it was what King Arthur would have eaten, but it looked good to him.

As he took his seat again, he could hardly believe that all their troubles were over. Prince was back safely with Max, and in the next few days the film would be finished. Meanwhile, they could all look forward to a real Arthurian Christmas.

No, he corrected himself, *a real doggy Christmas.* Because Christmas wouldn't be the same without dogs to share it. Briefly he felt a pang of unhappiness that Jake's dad Sam wasn't with him any more, but he knew that the best thing he could do for Sam's memory was to give everything he could to the dogs who were here.

But where's Princess? he wondered again.

As the thought crossed his mind, he heard a high-pitched yap from across the table. Princess poked her head up from where she was sitting on Max's lap, and put both forepaws on the white cloth as if she was waiting to be served.

"Max . . . " his mother said, laughing.

Max looked apologetic. "Well, it is Christmas. And she tracked Prince down. We wouldn't be enjoying this now if it wasn't for Princess. She did it all!"

"Sure she did," said Neil. "If anybody deserves a Christmas dinner, it's Princess. She's a real star!"

Holly's Wish

Chapter One

"Come on, Jake!" Neil Parker called to his young black-and-white Border collie as he tramped through the snow to the top of the ridgeway. He stopped to look back, and laughed at Jake's antics. The young dog was racing to and fro, trying to catch the whirling snowflakes in his mouth. Below them lay the snowy roofs of the small country town of Compton.

"Hurry up!" Emily, Neil's ten-year-old sister, called impatiently from further up the slope. "At this rate the snow will have melted before we get to the top."

Neil laughed. "There's not much chance of that," he said as he ran to catch up with her, dragging his sledge behind him. Neil had woken up that morning to find a carpet of deep snow covering the yard and roof-tops of King Street Kennels, the dog kennels and rescue centre that his parents, Bob and Carole Parker, ran. It had continued to snow steadily all morning and Neil hoped it would last until Christmas, which was only a week away.

He gazed up at the sky, narrowing his eyes against the dancing flakes, then smiled with satisfaction. The clouds looked heavy and grey, and Neil was sure there was still plenty of snow to come.

"Come on!" Emily called again. "Everyone else is there already. We don't want to miss all the fun." She turned and hurried up the hill with her sledge, her feet sinking into the snow at every step.

Neil whistled for Jake, then followed Emily, scanning the hillside above as he walked. It was crowded with sledgers and, even from this distance, Neil could identify quite a few of them. Chris Wilson and Hasheem Lindon, Neil's best friends from school, were trudging along the top of the ridgeway with a sledge. Toby and Amanda Sparrow were there too, with their young Dalmatian, Scrap. Steve Tansley, Neil's cousin, was involved in a snowball fight with a group of friends while his wayward Labrador, Ricky, charged backwards and forwards through the snow, barking with excitement.

"Look at Ben," Emily giggled as they climbed. "There's more snow on his coat than there is on the ground." Ben was an Old English sheepdog who belonged to Emily's best friend, Julie.

Neil grinned, then looked back at Jake again. The collie had almost caught up with them and his fur was caked in snow too. "Here, Jake," Neil called, crouching down. "You look like a snow dog!"

Jake hurtled towards him, sending flurries of loose snow flying up behind him. He cannoned into Neil, knocking him over. "Get off!" chuckled Neil, gently pushing the collie off him and scrambling to his feet. He caught hold of Jake's collar and brushed the worst of the snow off his coat while the Border collie nuzzled him with his wet nose. Neil gave him a dog treat from the supply he always carried in his pocket and Jake crunched it eagerly. Then the young dog raced ahead up the hill with an excited bark.

"Here's the Puppy Patrol!" called Hasheem as Neil and Emily reached the top of the hill. He

grinned at Neil. "Hey, haven't you got a special doggy sledge for Jake to ride on?"

Neil laughed. "He wouldn't bring his own sledge, Hasheem. He wanted to sit on your lap and ride down." He whistled and Jake came bounding up, ready to play.

"No way!" cried Hasheem, backing away in mock terror. Neil scooped up a handful of snow, shaped it into a snowball and threw it at Hasheem. It hit his chest, leaving a snowy mark. Hasheem laughed and hurled one back but his aim was wide of the mark and he hit Chris instead. In moments, a full-scale snowball fight had broken out.

"Is this a private fight or can anyone join in?" asked Julie, running up with Ben at her heels.

"The more, the merrier," laughed Emily, throwing a snowball at Julie then diving out of the way as her friend hurled one back. Ben and Jake dashed around wildly, leaping up to catch the snowballs as they rocketed over their heads.

"Yuck," Chris panted after a while, brushing snow off his clothes so that it showered around his feet. "My gloves are soaked." He peeled them off and shook them out.

"Does anyone want a sledge race?" Emily asked.

"You bet!" Neil whooped.

They all ran to fetch their sledges and positioned them at the top of the slope. Jake and Ben watched with interest, and Neil began to wonder whether Hasheem's suggestion that Jake should have a sledge of his own wasn't such a bad idea after all. The young Border collie would probably enjoy skimming down the hillside faster than he could run.

"Ready, steady, go!" cried Neil, and they pushed off.

"Last one down has to give us all a piggy back

to the top!" Julie shrieked as they raced downhill.

The ridgeway was perfect for tobogganing. The slope was long enough and steep enough to allow sledges to build up speed, but it levelled out at the bottom so that it was easy to stop. As he zoomed down, Neil could hear Jake barking loudly behind him. But the Border collie couldn't keep up with the speeding sledge and when Neil glanced back over his shoulder he saw Jake bounding after Ben instead, in a boisterous game of chase.

Julie reached the bottom of the hill first. Neil arrived a moment later, with Emily close behind him. Chris and Hasheem were last, slowed down because they were sharing a sledge.

"That was ace!" Neil cried, jumping up. "Let's have another go." He grinned at Chris and Hasheem. "Of course, as you two came last you'll have to give us all a piggy back to the top."

"No chance!" Hasheem yelled, darting a little way up hill.

They trailed back to the top of the hill, towing their sledges and talking excitedly about Christmas. Jake and Ben charged over to meet them, barking greetings.

"Come on, Chris," said Hasheem. "If we get

away quickly, we might win this time." He and Chris jumped on to their sledge and shot away. Neil, Emily and Julie quickly pulled their sledges into position. Jake gave an excited bark, then caught the rope of Neil's sledge in his teeth. "Let go, Jake!" Neil said. "Do you want me to be last this time?"

Jake dropped the rope, then raced around Neil's sledge instead. By the time Neil was ready to go, Julie and Emily were already halfway down the hill and Chris and Hasheem were nearly at the bottom. "Typical! Who'd have a dog?" Neil said, ruffling Jake's ears affectionately. Jake wagged his tail furiously and licked Neil's cheek.

"Mind out of the way then, Jake," said Neil, gently shoving the Border collie to one side. He pushed off with his feet and streaked away down the slope.

Suddenly Neil saw a dark shape in the snow ahead of him, directly in his path. He squinted through the snowflakes, trying to work out what it was. Then he realized, and his heart lurched. It was a Labrador puppy and, from what he could see, it was not very old.

"Look out!" Neil yelled. Frantically, he dug his heels into the snow, trying to slow his descent, but the sledge swept on as fast as ever, and the puppy didn't move. It watched, wide-eyed with apprehension, as Neil sped towards it.

Neil hauled on the rope. He had to change direction. If he hit the pup, it would be badly hurt. The nose of the sledge inched round. Neil jerked harder and the sledge swerved to the left.

To his relief, he realized that he was just going to miss the puppy – if it stayed where it was. But now Neil was heading for a prickly holly bush. He jerked on the rope again. This time it was too late. Shutting his eyes and throwing up his arms to protect his face, he hurtled straight into the bush.

Chapter Two

The branches lashed Neil as he barged into the holly bush, their prickly leaves snatching at his clothes. A branch caught in the collar of his coat and he tumbled into the snow.

He lay still for a moment, looking up at the dark glossy leaves and scarlet berries above his head. One of his gloves had been torn off in the crash and there was a long scratch on the back of his hand. Neil flexed his arms and legs, checking that he hadn't broken any bones. Then he rolled over and sat up.

"Neil!" Emily's frightened voice reached him from the bottom of the hill. "Are you all right?"

"Neil!" Chris yelled. "Where are you, mate?"

"Over here," called Neil. "I'm OK." He crawled out of the bush.

Jake hurtled down the slope, sending snow sliding ahead of him. He stood in front of Neil and looked at him enquiringly with his head on one side.

"It's OK, boy," Neil said, hugging the Border collie. "I'm not hurt."

Ben arrived a moment later and flopped down in the snow beside Jake with his tongue lolling. Neil patted him too.

Emily came charging up the hill, her face pink from running, with Chris, Hasheem and Julie close behind. "Are you all right?" she panted anxiously.

"Fine," said Neil as he got to his feet. "Apart from a few scratches and a lost glove, anyway. Is the puppy OK?" The Labrador was still standing above them on the slope, chest-deep in snow. It was watching them with huge brown eyes, its chocolate-brown coat speckled with snowflakes.

Hasheem laughed. "There's nothing wrong with you if you're worrying about dogs again!"

"The puppy looks OK," said Emily. "But why on earth is it on its own?"

"That's what I'd like to know too," Neil said

hotly. "It's too young to be out of doors in weather like this." He set off up the slope towards the puppy, with the others trailing after him. "The poor little thing must be frozen. I'd really like to hear what the owners have got to say about—" He broke off suddenly. "Hang on! Isn't it Holly, one of the Labrador puppies from the litter at the rescue centre? It looks exactly like her. And it's the right size."

"It does look like her," Emily agreed, "though I'm not one hundred per cent sure."

"What, she's one of those tiny puppies that were living in a box in your kitchen for a while?" asked Chris. "I fed one of them once when I came over to your house. It was a little black one."

Neil nodded. "That's right." The Parkers had hand-reared the four tiny Labradors after they had been found abandoned in the woods on the far side of Compton. They were only a few days old when they were rescued, and they had lived in the kitchen until they were big enough to move into the rescue centre.

"I fed them a couple of times too," Julie said. "They were really sweet." She looked at the puppy again. "Are they all as big as this one now?"

"One of the black ones, Santa, is a bit smaller," said Neil. He signalled to everyone to slow down as they drew closer to the Labrador pup. It was important to approach her quietly so that they didn't frighten her. He placed a restraining hand on Jake's collar. "Can you hang on to Ben, Julie?" he asked.

Julie grabbed hold of the Old English sheepdog.

"Someone left the puppies to die," Emily explained to Hasheem. "The owner dumped them in a bag in the middle of nowhere."

"That's terrible!" said Hasheem angrily. "What an awful thing to do!"

"They could easily have died of cold," Emily went on, with a shiver.

"Or starvation," Neil added gravely.

"I can't imagine anyone being that cruel," said Chris.

"We don't get many cases as bad as that," Emily said. "And luckily the puppies were found quite quickly by a man who was out walking his dog. He brought them straight to King Street Kennels."

"The Puppy Patrol to the rescue again!" Hasheem said. "What on earth would dogs do without the Parkers and their rescue centre?"

"Wait here now," Neil said over his shoulder. "The puppy will be scared if we all get too close." He clipped on Jake's lead and thrust it into Emily's hand. "Stay, Jake," he told the Border collie. Then he edged forward cautiously so that the Labrador wouldn't run off. "Holly," he called softly.

"Holly! Very appropriate," Hasheem joked, "seeing as you've just wrecked a holly bush, Neil, with your crazy sledge run."

They all started to laugh but Neil turned and placed a warning finger on his lips. "Don't scare her," he whispered, and the laughter quickly died away. "Holly," Neil called again. "Here, Holly. Good girl."

At the sound of her name, the Labrador puppy pricked up her ears and wagged her tiny tail feebly.

"I *knew* it was her," said Neil.

"Julie and I will fetch the sledges while you get hold of Holly," Emily said. "We'll take Jake and Ben with us, just in case they bother her. Come on, you two, let's go," she called to the dogs.

Holly watched Neil with a trusting expression as he advanced. At last he was close enough to touch her. He reached out a hand, letting her

sniff his bare skin, then he lifted her into his arms. "Good girl," he said soothingly.

The puppy snuggled against him, shivering. "Poor thing, you're frozen," said Neil, brushing snow off Holly's glossy coat. She was wearing a red leather collar with an identity disc. Neil twisted the collar round until he could read the disc. The name *Morgan* was inscribed on it, with a telephone number underneath.

"Is it definitely Holly?" Chris asked, moving forward and holding out his hand to the young Labrador. She craned forward to sniff him, then sank back against Neil's chest again, with a weary sigh.

"Yes." Neil unzipped his coat and tucked the shivering pup inside. "It says Morgan on her identity disc. That's the name of the people who adopted her."

"Is she going to be all right, mate?" asked Chris, gently stroking her chin with one finger. Holly twisted her head and licked his glove with a tiny pink tongue.

Neil was relieved to feel her tail thud against his chest – she was obviously feeling better already. "She's just cold, scared and worn out," he said. "But she'll be fine when she's warmed up and had a rest."

Emily and Julie clambered up the hill, pulling the sledges. Jake was off the lead now and he was carrying Neil's missing glove in his mouth. He dropped it at Neil's feet, then sat down proudly, his wagging tail sweeping the loose snow from side to side.

"Well done, Jake," Neil praised. He felt in his pocket for a dog treat but the packet wasn't there.

Emily laughed. "I don't think Jake should have any more treats. He found the packet under the bush while he was searching for your glove and wolfed most of them!"

"Ben helped him as well," giggled Julie.

Neil grinned and patted the Border collie's head. Then he pulled the glove on gratefully, suddenly realizing how chilled his hand was.

"What are we going to do with her?" asked Emily, fondling Holly's ears.

Neil scanned the hillside. "Nobody seems to be looking for her so we'd better take her back to her home. Her owners live in one of those old cottages that back on to the ridgeway. I remember thinking it was an ideal place for a dog—" He broke off, frowning. Once again, he tried to imagine what sort of people would let a young puppy wander off alone in the snow. His mum and dad always checked that rescue dogs were going to good homes but perhaps they'd made a mistake this time. . .

"Have you found homes for the other Labrador puppies?" asked Julie as they trudged along the ridgeway. She stroked the top of Holly's head and Neil felt the puppy's tail wagging again inside his coat.

"No, the other three are still at the rescue centre," he said.

Julie frowned. "You'd think loads of people would want to adopt gorgeous little creatures like this."

Holly gave a tiny high-pitched bark, as

though she'd understood what Julie said and fully agreed.

"I'm sure we'll find homes for the others soon," said Neil. "I want to see them all settled by Christmas."

Chris whistled. "Do you reckon you'll do it? Homing three puppies in a week is pushing it a bit, isn't it, mate?"

Neil squared his shoulders determinedly. "We'll do it."

They reached the end of the ridgeway. Low-roofed, old-fashioned cottages were clearly visible through the leafless trees ahead. Neil and Emily said goodbye to Chris, Hasheem and Julie, and set off along a narrow path that led between two of the cottages to the quiet road beyond. Jake and Ben touched noses, then Jake trotted quickly after Neil.

It didn't take long to find Ridgeview Cottage, the Morgans' house. Neil marched up to the front door and rang the bell, with Emily and Jake close behind.

A plump, anxious-looking woman opened the door. "Mrs Morgan?" Emily asked politely.

The woman nodded. "That's right." Suddenly she caught sight of the puppy peeping out from inside Neil's coat and her face lit up. "Holly!

Thank goodness! We've been looking every-where for you," she said before Neil had a chance to speak. She held out her hands and Neil placed Holly in her arms.

"It's all right, girl," he said soothingly. "You're home now."

"She is all right, isn't she?" Mrs Morgan asked, concerned.

"She seems fine – just a bit scared," Neil said. "Er. . . why exactly was she out on her own?"

"I let her out in the garden," said Mrs Morgan. "I thought it was safe. When I went to fetch her a couple of minutes later she just wasn't there. There must be a hole in the fence." She hugged the little puppy. "I've been so worried about her."

Mrs Morgan ushered Neil, Emily and Jake inside. "Thank you so much for bringing her home," she said, leading the way into a large, welcoming kitchen at the front of the house. "My husband's still out searching for her – he'll be so relieved."

A log fire was burning cheerfully at one end of the kitchen, its flickering flames casting an orange glow across the flagstone floor. Mrs Morgan crossed to a large airing cupboard and took out a pink, fluffy towel. Then she sat down in a chair, cradled Holly on her lap and rubbed her dry.

"Would you like to sit down?" Mrs Morgan asked, smiling up at Neil and Emily.

They settled down on the big, comfortable sofa, while Jake lay down by the fire. Neil relaxed. He'd been angry with the Morgans for letting Holly roam free but now it seemed that he'd made a mistake. Mrs Morgan was clearly just as concerned about the Labrador as he was.

"She's a smashing little pup," said Neil, watching the Labrador, who had curled up on Mrs Morgan's lap and was dozing contentedly.

"Yes, Holly's going to be our daughter's dog," explained Mrs Morgan. "We only moved here two weeks ago and a few days before that our dog died." She sighed. "We'd had her for sixteen years and we all miss her badly, but our daughter Alex is heartbroken."

They heard a door open at the back of the house. "I can't find her anywhere," a man's worried voice called. "I've been all over the ridgeway but—"

"It's all right, John," Mrs Morgan interrupted. "Holly's home. Some kind people have brought her back." She turned to Neil. "How did you know where to bring Holly?"

"We recognized her and then saw your name on her collar," explained Neil. "Our parents own King Street Kennels and I remember them saying that Holly's new owners lived here."

Mrs Morgan smiled. "You must be Neil, then. Alex is going to be in your class at school. And you must be Emily. Your dad told me all about you two."

A tall, smiling man came into the room. He was still wearing his coat and hat and his face was red with cold. "What a relief!" He took off his gloves and patted Holly affectionately. She lifted her head and blinked at him, then fell asleep again. "Thanks for bringing her home. Where did you find her?"

"Up on the ridgeway. We were sledging there," said Emily. "In fact, we're going back there now. Do you think Alex would like to come with us?"

"It's kind of you to ask, Emily," Mrs Morgan said. "I'm sure she'd love to, but she's not here. She's been staying at her grandparents' in Manchester since we moved so she could finish the term at her old school." She glanced at her watch. "I thought they'd have arrived by now, though," she added. "Her gran's bringing her over. Perhaps the snow's held them up."

"She doesn't know about Holly yet," explained Mr Morgan. "But she'll be really excited when she meets her." As he spoke, a red car drew up outside. "At last! Here they are," he said. "I'll go and let them in."

Neil and Emily watched through the window as Alex and her grandmother came up the snowy path, each carrying a suitcase. Alex was tall and skinny, with long dark hair pulled back into a ponytail. She wasn't wearing a coat and the falling snow speckled her black jumper. She looked just like a Dalmatian in reverse, Neil thought, grinning to himself.

Holly opened her eyes and sat up, refreshed by her nap. Mrs Morgan put her down on the floor. "Alex is coming, girl," she said.

Holly wagged her tail and gave a tiny bark. Jake stood up, obviously intending to go and make friends with the puppy, but Neil told him to stay and the Border collie sat down again obediently.

Neil heard Mr Morgan say hello to his daughter. "Go through into the kitchen, Alex," he continued. "We've got a surprise for you."

Alex appeared in the doorway, followed by her dad and her gran. "Hello, love," said Mrs

Morgan, giving her a hug. "Meet Holly. She's your new dog."

Alex's smile faded. She stared at Holly in horror. "How could you? I don't want a new dog," she cried, and burst into tears.

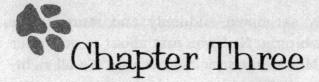

Chapter Three

"If I can't have Daisy I don't want any dog," sobbed Alex. "Don't you understand that?"

"But Daisy's not with us any more, love," Mrs Morgan said gently. She tried to put her arms round her daughter, but Alex pulled away.

Holly trotted towards Alex, her tail wagging and her mouth open in a welcoming grin. "Look, she likes you already," Mr Morgan said encouragingly.

Alex shook her head. "I don't want her. I'm never having another dog." She stumbled out of the room with tears pouring down her cheeks. Her gran followed her, calling to her to come back.

Holly sat down suddenly and stared after Alex, whining. Neil was just about to go to her when Mrs Morgan picked her up. "It's all right, Holly," she said reassuringly, stroking the puppy who nestled against her.

Neil knew how Alex was feeling. When his own dog, Sam, had died, he'd been devastated. But at least he'd had Jake, Sam's son, to ease the pain. He bent down to stroke Jake, running his hand over the Border collie's coat and letting Jake nuzzle his neck. It was never easy when a dog died, he thought, but in the end you had to move on. There were so many other dogs in need of a loving home.

"Oh dear," said Mr Morgan, staring after Alex in dismay. "What on earth are we going to do now?"

"I really don't know." Mrs Morgan's shoulders slumped. "I was sure she'd fall in love with Holly the moment she saw her."

There was an awkward silence.

"Look," said Neil, "if you like, we could take Holly back to the rescue centre – just for the moment."

The Morgans exchanged worried glances. "Perhaps it would be best," Mr Morgan said hesitantly.

"She'll be back with her brothers and sister," Neil pointed out.

"And maybe Alex will change her mind," added Emily. "After all, how could she resist such a gorgeous little pup?"

"I hope you're right," Mr Morgan said.

Mrs Morgan shook her head firmly. "I'm sure Alex will realize she wants her soon. She's probably thinking it over right now."

"But you know how stubborn she can be sometimes," Mr Morgan reminded her.

Mrs Morgan bit her lip. "I know. But poor Holly. She's such a lovely puppy. *I* don't like the idea of having to part with her." She hugged the Labrador tightly.

"We just need to give Alex a bit of space," Mr Morgan said. He reached out for Holly, and Mrs Morgan handed her over reluctantly. "She may well decide she wants to keep her in a day or two," Mr Morgan reassured his wife, "but it'll be best if Holly's not here reminding Alex of Daisy while she's getting used to the idea of having another dog."

Mrs Morgan gave a weak smile. "I know you're right, John," she said. "But all the same . . ." She gave Holly one last stroke then turned to Neil. "I'll fetch her things." She

271

hurried out of the room, returning a few moments later with a dog carrier, a soft blue blanket and a squeaky rubber bone.

Emily spread the blanket in the bottom of the dog carrier. "This will keep Holly warm on the way home," she said.

Neil took Holly from Mr Morgan and put her inside the carrier. "Good girl," he said as she snuggled into the blanket. He put the rubber bone beside her and shut the door, checking that the catch was fastened properly. "Don't worry. We'll take good care of her," he promised, straightening up. He called Jake to heel and picked up the dog carrier. Then he, Emily and Jake went back out into the snow.

"Thanks for all your help," Mrs Morgan called after them.

Neil and Emily waved as they set off. Emily pulled both sledges behind her while Neil carried Holly. "Poor thing," he said. "Let's hope Alex decides she wants her soon. If not, we're going to have to find homes for *four* puppies before Christmas!"

A grey Morris Minor was turning into King Street Kennels as Neil, Emily and Jake arrived home with Holly. "It's Gavin and Jet," Emily said. Gavin Thorpe was the young vicar of Compton and Jet, his black Labrador, always stayed at King Street Kennels when Gavin and his wife Susie went on holiday.

"I wonder if he'd like one of the Labrador puppies to keep Jet company," said Neil thoughtfully.

Emily shook her head. "I shouldn't think so. Susie's going to have her baby soon. I can hardly see her and Gavin wanting a baby and a puppy."

"Yeah, I suppose it would be difficult," Neil agreed.

The Morris Minor came to a stop on the snowy drive. Gavin climbed out and Jet jumped out after him. "Hello, you two. Lovely day," Gavin joked, looking wryly at the sky.

"Hello, Gavin," Neil and Emily said together.

Jet trotted towards them, tail wagging and eyes bright. "Hi, Jet," Neil said, running a hand over his smooth fur. He put the dog carrier down, opened its wire door and lifted Holly out, still wrapped in her blanket. Jet stretched up to sniff her. She peeped out of her blanket, her dark eyes wary as she looked at the newcomer.

"It's OK, Holly," said Neil, giving her a comforting stroke.

Emily crouched down to make a fuss of Jet and he licked her cheek affectionately. Then he turned his attention to Jake. The two dogs touched noses briefly, before launching into a boisterous game of chase that involved racing round and round Gavin's car and occasionally wriggling underneath it and out the other side.

"Have you come to book Jet in for a holiday?" asked Emily.

"Not this time," said the vicar. Jet ran back to him and Gavin ruffled his glossy black fur. "Actually I've come to ask your dad a huge favour."

"You'd better come in then," Neil said. He and Emily ushered Gavin round the side of the house and into the Parkers' kitchen. The house was warm and bright, and smelt deliciously of spicy mincemeat. A Christmas song was playing on the radio.

Carole was bending over the kitchen table, rolling out pastry. Sarah, Neil and Emily's five-year-old sister, was helping her, squeezing pastry scraps into Christmassy shapes. "I'm making an angel and Father Christmas and a stocking," she said proudly, holding up one of the shapes to show them. Her eyes widened as Holly poked her head out of the blanket. "A puppy!" she squealed, delighted. Dropping the pastry, she hurried across to Neil.

Carole Parker looked up. "Hello, Gavin," she said. "Come and sit down while I see what Neil's up to." She shot Neil a questioning glance.

"Thanks," said Gavin. He unbuttoned his coat and sat down, while Jet settled contentedly at his feet.

Carole pushed a strand of dark hair out of her face with the back of one floury hand, leaving a white streak across her forehead, then turned to Neil. "Where on earth have you got that puppy from?"

"It's Holly," Neil said gloomily, and he and Emily explained what had happened.

"You were right to bring her back," sighed Carole. She brushed flour off her hands then came to look at the puppy. "I wouldn't like to think of her belonging to someone who didn't want her," she added, rubbing the side of the pup's head with one finger. Holly stuck out a small, pink tongue and licked Carole's hand. "Poor Alex. I can understand why she'd feel like that. It's very hard to lose a dog you love. But perhaps she'll come round."

"I hope so," said Neil. He was sure Holly was just what Alex needed.

"We could keep Holly," Sarah said eagerly, stretching up on tiptoe to stroke the puppy. "She gets on really well with Jake and—"

"We are not having another dog," Carole said firmly.

"But she's really sweet—" wailed Sarah.

"No!" said Carole.

"Do you want us to put her back in the rescue centre?" asked Neil. He wished they could keep Holly but he knew it would be pointless to try to talk his mother round.

"Yes, please," Carole said. As she turned to Gavin, Jake trotted across to her and rubbed against her leg, soaking her jeans. "Jake!" she groaned.

"Yeah, he's pretty wet from being out in the snow," said Neil. "Could you give him a rub down, please? And can you make sure his feet are dry."

Carole laughed. "I do know how to look after dogs, Neil."

Neil laughed too. "Sorry."

In spite of the snow outside, the rescue centre felt deliciously warm when Neil and Emily went in. "I'll prepare a bowl of food for her," said Emily. "She must be starving after being out in the cold for so long."

"Good idea," Neil said. He fetched a towel and gently rubbed Holly's head – the only part of her that had been exposed to the weather when she'd been out of the dog carrier. By the time she was dry, her fur was standing up in chocolate-brown spikes. Neil smoothed it down, then set the puppy beside the bowl of food that Emily had prepared. She tucked in hungrily.

When she'd finished eating, Neil carried her to the pen that her sister and brothers shared. The pups were in their basket, lying asleep in a contented heap. Holly whined and wagged her tail as she picked up their scent. The puppies stirred.

"Come on, you lazy lot. Wake up and say hello to your sister," Neil called as Emily unfastened the door. The smallest puppy, a black Labrador who they had named Santa, struggled out from underneath his heavier golden sister, Candy, and darted to the wire. He eyed Holly inquisitively, his tail swinging from side to side.

Neil carried Holly into the pen and set her down. In seconds the other three puppies, two black and one golden, were all around her, sniffing her, touching noses and welcoming her home. Then the four of them plunged into a wild and joyful game of chase.

Neil watched with mixed emotions. It was good that the puppies were pleased to see Holly but he couldn't help feeling sorry for her. The rescue centre was warm and comfortable but it wasn't nearly as nice as the Morgans' house. She'd miss the attention that the Morgans had given her too, Neil thought. He made up his mind to visit her as often as he could.

Gavin, Carole and Bob were chatting and drinking coffee when Neil and Emily went indoors. Jake and Jet were lying by the stove.

Jake sprang up and trotted across to Neil, leaping up to lick his face.

"Down, boy," Neil commanded.

Jake sat down obediently, watching Neil intently, his bright eyes sparkling.

"You've got him well trained," said Gavin admiringly.

Neil laughed. "Most of the time. But he has his moments, don't you, Jake?" The Border collie barked in response.

"Anyway, Gavin, can we do something for you, or is this just a social visit?" Bob asked.

"I'm after some help, I'm afraid," said the vicar.

Bob stroked his beard thoughtfully. "I'll help out if I can, but we're a bit pushed for time today. Bev and Kate aren't working and this snow means that simple jobs take twice as long." Bev and Kate were King Street Kennels' hard-working and committed kennel maids.

Gavin nodded. "The snow's caused problems on the roads, too. I hope it's not going to take me too long to get home – I don't like leaving Susie on her own." He produced a mobile phone from his pocket and checked that it was switched on. "She's going to ring me if anything happens. The baby's due in ten days' time."

Carole smiled. "You must be really excited."

"I can't wait," Gavin said. "Our first son or daughter!"

"So do you want me to drive you both to the hospital in the Range Rover when the time comes?" asked Bob.

Gavin shook his head. "It's not that. It's rather an unusual favour actually." Neil thought he looked slightly embarrassed. "You see, I'm going to set up a Christmas grotto in the church hall – for children and dogs."

"That sounds ace!" Neil cried.

Bob laughed. "A Christmas grotto for dogs?" He put down his empty coffee mug. "It's an original idea – I'll give you that."

"We've got to raise some money to get the church hall roof repaired," said Gavin. "There are so many dogs in Compton I thought that people might be willing to pay a small amount to bring their kids *and* their dogs to see Father Christmas."

"I'll bring Jake," said Neil. "He'll love seeing all his doggy friends." He ruffled the Border collie's ears and Jake's tail thumped rhythmically on the floor. "Loads of people will come. Doctor Harvey will bring Finn and Sandy—" Neil began.

"And Julie and Ben will come," Emily chipped in. "And Steve and Ricky."

"I bet Mrs Jepson will bring Sugar and Spice," said Neil, with a laugh. "In fact, she'll probably bring them four times at least." Sugar and Spice were the most pampered pooches in Compton.

"So where does Bob come into this?" asked Carole.

Gavin blushed slightly and twisted his empty coffee mug round and round. "I was hoping you'd dress up as Father Christmas, Bob," he mumbled.

Neil, Emily and Carole all laughed.

"Father Christmas! Me?" Bob shook his head. "You are joking?"

"No. You'd be perfect. You've got a real way with dogs," the vicar insisted.

"Well maybe. . . But what about the kids?" asked Bob.

Gavin smiled. "Oh I'm sure they'll be as good as gold. Will you do it?"

"I don't know . . ." Bob began, pulling a face.

"Oh go on, Dad," cried Emily. "You'd be brilliant."

"You'd look great in that red suit," Neil chuckled. "You might have to dye your beard, though."

Sarah came into the kitchen, carrying her hamster, Fudge, in her cupped hands. She was frowning. "Shhh," she said crossly. "I'm trying to teach Fudge to dance. He wants to be a ballerina, like me." Sarah thought her hamster was the cleverest creature in the world.

Neil started to laugh, then hastily changed it into a cough as Sarah turned a furious face towards him. "How's he getting on, Squirt?" he asked.

"He was doing really well until you all started laughing and putting him off," huffed Sarah.

"What's so funny, anyway?"

"Dad's going to dress up as Father Christmas and give out presents to dogs and children," Emily explained.

"Why can't the real Father Christmas do it?" asked Sarah.

"He's too busy," said Gavin. "But he's quite happy for your dad to stand in for him." The vicar turned to Bob. "So will you do it?"

"Of course he will," Carole said quickly. "And he'll enjoy every minute of it."

"There's your answer, then," said Bob with a grin. "If Carole says I'll do it, then I'll do it."

"Excellent." Gavin beamed at him. "I've got a big sack of presents in the boot of my car. I was wondering whether you and Emily might be able to wrap them for me, Neil?"

"We'd love to," Emily said eagerly.

"I'll give you a hand bringing them in," offered Neil.

The vicar stood up. "Thanks for the coffee, Carole. And thanks for agreeing to stand in for Father Christmas, Bob," he said with a wink. He called to Jet and the black Labrador stood up and stretched.

"Let us know as soon as there's any news about the baby," said Carole.

"I will. See you soon."

The vicar followed Neil outside. It was still snowing; large white flakes curled thickly down from the heavy grey sky. The tracks that Neil and Emily had left when they had come in from the rescue centre were already half filled with snow. Neil tilted his head back so that the snow settled on his face. A few flakes drifted into his open mouth and he let them melt on his tongue.

While Gavin unlocked the boot of his Morris Minor, Neil watched Jake and Jet. The two dogs slid along the ground on their tummies, pushing the snow into heaps with their noses and front paws. Then they rolled over, barking excitedly, and leapt up again, sending the snow flying up in wild flurries.

Neil groaned. "Typical! Now Jake will have to be dried again."

Gavin lifted a black bin bag out of his boot. "Here you are, Neil. Thanks for agreeing to wrap them." He opened the car door and Jet darted across to him and jumped inside. The Labrador scrambled over the front seats and flopped down on a rug in the back. "Bye, Neil," Gavin called as he started the engine. "Good luck with those pups. I hope you manage to find homes for all of them."

"Thanks! I'm sure we will," Neil said cheerfully. But he didn't feel quite so sure. If they were going to find homes for Holly and her brothers and sister before Christmas, they'd need all the luck they could get.

Chapter Four

"I wish Gavin had bought presents that were easier to wrap," Emily said, pulling a rubber bone out of the plastic sack on the floor. "Some of these things are really fiddly."

"If you think that's difficult, have a go at one of these," said Neil, waving a pyramid-shaped puzzle at her and making the balls inside it rattle. They were sitting at the kitchen table, wrapping presents for the Christmas grotto. Jake lay stretched out on his side in front of the stove, basking in the heat.

"Hey, why don't we phone Jake Fielding about the puppies?" Emily suggested suddenly. Jake was the young reporter for the *Compton*

News and he'd helped the Parkers out before, when they'd needed publicity for their rescue dogs. "That article he did about them in the paper when they were first found was brilliant. I'm sure he'd do another one about them needing homes – and take their pictures. I bet loads of people would want to adopt them, then."

"Brilliant, Em!" said Neil. "Let's ring him straight away. And we could make posters and put them up around Compton."

"Yes. We should put an ad on the King Street Kennels' website too."

Neil finished wrapping the pyramid puzzle then fetched the bin bag and held it open by the edge of the table. "Slide the wrapped presents in here, then we'll ask Mum if we can use the office computer," he said to Emily.

They hurried to the office and found Carole hard at work on the computer.

"Oh, we were going to make some posters advertising the puppies," Neil explained, looking disappointed. "I suppose we can come back later if you're busy."

Carole shook her head and sighed. "I've had enough of office work for the moment – I'm exhausted now. The computer's all yours."

It didn't take long to make the posters. "They're nice and bright," Emily said approvingly as she took the first one out of the printer. She read it out: "*Wanted: good homes for gorgeous Labrador puppies. Apply to King Street Kennels, Compton.*" Underneath this heading was a photo of the puppies that they'd scanned into the computer. Neil had taken it the day before the puppies had moved from the Parkers' kitchen to the rescue centre. They were all sitting on the rug, gazing at the camera appealingly.

Neil phoned Jake Fielding while the posters were printing, and the reporter promised to come over the next day to take the puppies' photo. He said he could probably get the story in that week's issue of the *Compton News*.

"Loads of people will see them in the paper," said Emily, when Neil had rung off and told her the good news. "I bet we'll get hundreds of people phoning about them."

Neil laughed. "We don't need hundreds. Only three. . . Or four," he added, "if Alex doesn't come back for Holly."

"Do you think she will come?" Emily asked.

Neil shrugged. "I hope so. Anyway, let's not worry about Alex now. We need to update the

King Street Kennels website." He connected to the Internet, then added the puppies' details and their photo to the website. "There," he said. "I just hope lots of people read it."

Neil and Emily put the posters into a plastic bag to keep them dry, then set off for Compton with Jake. It had stopped snowing but there was no sign of a thaw. They walked quickly, their footsteps muffled by the deep snow that covered the pavement. "I hope this weather lasts," said Neil as they turned into the high street. "A white Christmas would be ace!"

Strings of coloured lights hung across the high street and most of the shops had a decorated tree in the window.

They reached the supermarket and Emily took a poster inside. When she came out again an assistant was already positioning it in the window. "Wow! It looks brilliant!" Neil whooped. "People will spot it from a mile off."

"No one will be able to resist having a puppy when they see that photo," said Emily.

They continued down the high street, taking posters into the greengrocer's and the shoe shop. Neil glanced back at them as he walked towards the baker's. "There are already people looking— Oof!" he gasped suddenly as he collided with someone and stumbled backwards.

Jake darted over and jumped up at him. He seemed to think Neil was playing a game. "Get off, you daft dog," Neil said. He gently pushed Jake down, and saw Alex standing beside him, holding a loaf of bread and grinning.

"Are you all right?" she asked.

"Fine. Was it you I bumped into?"

"Yes. But it's OK. You've only dented my loaf a bit," Alex laughed, bending down to stroke Jake. "Your dog's lovely," she said, rubbing his head. "What's his name?"

"This is Jake," Emily said.

Neil watched her making a fuss of the young Border collie. It was obvious that she loved dogs and he wished that he could persuade her to take Holly. The two of them would be good for each other.

"We've made some posters advertising the puppies," said Neil. "Do you want to give us a hand with them? We're trying to persuade shopkeepers to display them." Perhaps helping to find homes for the puppies would make Alex realize that she did want Holly after all, he thought.

Alex looked doubtful. "I don't think . . ." she began hesitantly.

"Oh go on," Neil pleaded, holding out a poster to her. "We could really do with some help, couldn't we, Em?"

Emily looked puzzled but she nodded anyway.

"All right, then." Alex took a poster. "Aren't they gorgeous?" she said, looking at their picture. "I should think everyone will—" She broke off and bit her lip, but Neil felt certain she'd been about to say that everyone would want to adopt one.

As soon as Alex took the poster into the baker's shop, Emily turned to Neil.

"Why were you so desperate for Alex to help?" she asked. "I mean, it's not as if we can't manage."

"I thought she'd be more likely to take Holly if she was involved in finding homes for the other puppies," he explained.

"Ah. . . nice idea," Emily said approvingly.

Alex reappeared a moment later, smiling broadly. "They're going to put it up."

"Brilliant!" said Neil. He handed Alex another poster. "Do you want to try the sweet shop next?"

They carried on through the centre of Compton until they had run out of posters.

"My grandad used to breed Shelties," Alex said as they turned to walk home. "He goes to loads of doggy events. If you print out some more posters I'll ask him to put them up in Manchester – if you like."

"That would be ace!" Emily said enthu-siastically. "The more people who hear about the puppies, the more chance we've got of finding homes for all of them."

Alex looked wistful for a moment. "Are they all good-natured?" she asked.

"Oh, yes," Emily said. "They've all got their own personalities. Santa's very sweet – he's the little black one. Candy, the golden one, is inquisitive, Cracker's really playful but Holly's the most friendly."

"Why don't you come and visit Holly at the rescue centre?" Neil suggested. "I'm sure she'd be glad to see you. And you could meet her brothers and sister too."

Alex shook her head unhappily. "No, thanks."

"I expect Holly will be feeling a bit lonely at the moment," Neil went on. "She lived with your mum and dad for four days so she's used to having people around her. She could definitely use some company." He didn't tell her that he was constantly popping into the rescue centre with Emily and Sarah to see the puppies. After spending so many weeks hand-rearing them in their kitchen, they all wanted to see as much of them as possible.

Alex shook her head again, more firmly this time. Her eyes were sad. "*Daisy* was my dog. I don't want another one." There was an awkward silence. Neil realized that persuading Alex to take Holly back wasn't going to be an easy task.

"Why don't you help us with the Christmas grotto at the church, then?" asked Emily, changing the subject. "We promised the vicar we'd wrap all the presents. We've made a start but there's loads more to do."

Alex frowned.

"Oh, go on," Neil said. "We'll never get them done on our own." *Perhaps we'll be able to persuade Alex to visit Holly once she is at King Street,* he thought hopefully.

Alex nodded. "All right," she agreed, looking a bit less miserable.

"Come round tomorrow morning," said Emily. "And—" She broke off suddenly as somebody called her name.

A blond boy was dashing towards them, weaving in and out of the shoppers on the pavement. "Emily! Hey, Emily!"

"It's Tom Charlton," Emily said. "He's in my class at school."

Tom pounded up to them, his face glowing with excitement, and skidded to a halt. "I saw your posters!" he panted. "I've just moved to a house with a garden and my mum and dad said I could have a dog. Will you save one of your puppies for me?"

"It's not quite as simple as that," Neil explained. "My parents will want to talk to your mum or dad before they let you have one of the puppies. But I'm sure it will be OK," he added quickly as he saw Tom's face fall. "When do you want to come?"

"How about tomorrow morning?" asked Tom eagerly.

"OK, come over at about half past ten," Neil said.

"You won't let them all go before then, will you?" Tom asked.

"No, of course not," Neil promised.

"I don't know which one I'll choose. They're all gorgeous," Tom said.

"They certainly are," Emily agreed.

"See you tomorrow then," said Tom. He raced away.

"Our poster campaign's working!" Emily cried, delighted. "At this rate *all* the puppies will be gone by Christmas."

Neil turned to speak to Alex but she wasn't there. "Hey, where's Alex gone?" he asked. He looked along the high street and saw her hurrying away with her head down. Neil guessed she was thinking about Daisy. But perhaps she was feeling guilty too, for rejecting Holly when Tom was obviously so enthusiastic about giving one of the pups a home. Or perhaps she was even worried that Tom might choose Holly.

"Poor Alex," said Emily. "She looks so unhappy."

"Holly would know how to cheer her up," said Neil. "We've just got to find a way of making her see it . . ."

Chapter Five

"The phone!" Neil cried, jumping up from the breakfast table next morning. "Perhaps it's somebody ringing about the puppies!"

Bob Parker laid a restraining hand on his arm. "I don't want you scaring a potential customer away by begging them to take one of the pups," he laughed, and went out of the room to answer it himself.

Neil sat down again. Jake, who was sitting beside him, watched hopefully as he bit into a slice of toast. "You've had your breakfast, Jake," Neil laughed.

The Border collie gave him a doggy grin and thumped the floor with his tail.

"That was Gavin, calling from the hospital," said Bob, reappearing in the kitchen doorway. "The baby's on the way now – over a week early. Poor Gavin's worried about the grotto, and he's asked if we could start decorating it later."

"Brilliant!" Emily cried.

"You bet!" whooped Neil.

"What about you, Sarah?" Carole asked. "Do you want to help decorate the Christmas grotto?"

Sarah shook her head. "No. I'm giving Fudge a dancing lesson. And I'm making a Christmas card for the puppies."

Bob drained his mug of tea. "That hamster must be the best dancer in the world." As he headed for the back door there was a knock on the front door. Emily hurried to answer it and came back with Alex.

"Oh I'm sorry," said Alex, looking at the breakfast table. "Have I come too early?"

"Of course not," Neil said, reaching for another slice of toast.

"Neil," Carole laughed. "Haven't you had enough yet?"

Neil shook his head. "Nearly. This is Alex, Mum. She's going to help us wrap the presents for the grotto."

"Hello, Alex. Would you like some breakfast?" Carole asked.

"No thanks," said Alex. "I've only just had mine."

"Nobody's phoned about the puppies yet," Neil said, while he and Emily cleared the kitchen table. "I visited them this morning. Holly seemed a bit miserable but she perked up when she saw me." He watched Alex as he spoke. She definitely looked interested when he mentioned Holly, and Neil was convinced that was a good sign.

They sat round the kitchen table and set to work wrapping presents. Jake watched them curiously for a while, then he flopped down by the stove for a nap.

"Perhaps you and I could take the money at the grotto, Alex," suggested Emily.

Alex smiled. "That'd be great! I might get to meet some people then. It's funny living in Compton and not knowing anyone. I had loads of friends in Manchester."

"I'll introduce you to some of my friends from school, if you like," said Neil. "You're going to be in my class so you'll get to know them soon anyway."

"I'd like that," Alex said, cutting off a length

299

of sticky tape. "By the way, I phoned my grandad last night and told him about the puppies. He said I could send him some posters – and he's going to ring his friends to see if they know anyone who wants a puppy."

"Ace!" Neil finished wrapping a squeaky dog ball and put the parcel on the growing pile in the centre of the table. "I'll print out some posters for you today."

Just then Neil heard the sound of a car turning into the drive. He looked out of the window to see who it was. "It's Tom and his dad," he told Emily and Alex. "They're bang on time – Tom really must be keen!"

As soon as Neil opened the door, Tom asked anxiously, "You have kept me a puppy, haven't you?"

Neil grinned. "Yes, don't worry." It was good to see somebody so genuinely enthusiastic about adopting a dog. Neil was already sure that Tom would make a good owner.

Tom's eyes lit up. "Brilliant," he said, following Neil across the yard to the rescue centre. "I've wanted a dog for ages and ages." He grinned at his dad, a friendly-looking man with short ginger hair. "Now I'm going to get one at last."

"Wait for us," Emily called as she and Alex came out of the house. "We're coming too!" Emily dashed after them, but Neil saw that Alex followed more slowly.

"How did you persuade her to come?" Neil whispered, when Emily caught up with him.

"I said I needed her to help me feed them." Emily grinned.

"Nice one!" said Neil.

Bob came out of Kennel Block One and shook hands with Mr Charlton. "You're interested in one of our Labrador pups, I hear," he said warmly.

"That's right," confirmed Mr Charlton.

"Come into the office and we'll discuss the details while Tom's choosing the puppy he thinks he'd like. Could you take Tom into the rescue centre, Neil?"

"Right." Neil led the way inside. Holly and Candy trotted up to the wire netting of their pen and watched as Neil, Emily and Tom approached. Santa and Cracker, the two black puppies, were curled up in their basket, side by side. Cracker opened an eye sleepily, then lumbered to his feet. Santa yawned lazily as he stood up and stretched.

"They're gorgeous!" Tom cried. He crouched down and pushed his fingers through the wire. The puppies crowded round, their tails wagging with excitement. Alex watched from a distance, her face tense and pale.

"There are two girls and two boys," said Neil. He opened the door of the pen and went inside, followed by Emily and Tom. Alex hung back at first, but Emily eventually persuaded her to come in. To Neil's delight, Holly rushed straight over to Alex, barking a greeting.

"She remembers you!" Emily said.

Alex nodded, frowning. She tried not to look at the puppy but Holly was clearly determined to be noticed. She scrambled on to Alex's foot and pawed at her leg, whining.

"Do you want to hold her?" asked Neil.

Alex shook her head, but she crouched down and rumpled Holly's silky ears. The puppy licked the inside of Alex's wrist, her tail lashing from side to side. Alex leant forward and spoke softly to Holly. Neil couldn't hear what she was saying but he was pleased to see that Alex's frown had faded.

The other three puppies wouldn't leave Tom alone. They banged each other aside in their determination to get his full attention. Eventually he sat down and let them clamber on to his lap. "They're fantastic!" he said, beaming at Neil and Emily. "They're just fantastic!"

He picked up Santa and held him against his chest. "But this one's the best of all. Look at his cute little face." The puppy nuzzled Tom's neck, then stretched up and licked his ear.

Tom laughed. "Hey, that tickles! I'd like this one, please. What's his name?"

"Santa," Emily said.

"That's perfect," said Tom.

Emily picked up the other two puppies, so Tom and Santa could get to know each other properly. Holly had pressed herself against

Alex's ankle and fallen asleep. Alex was still stroking her. Neil felt frustrated. He wouldn't dream of trying to get Alex to take Holly if he thought she couldn't cope with her, but it was clear that a bond was growing between the two of them.

The outer door of the rescue centre opened and Bob and Mr Charlton came in. "All the paperwork's done," Bob announced. "It looks like you and your family will make very good dog owners, Tom."

Tom grinned and stood up, holding Santa carefully. "I've chosen this one, Dad. He's called Santa. Can we take him home now?"

"I'll fetch the dog carrier from the car," Mr Charlton laughed.

Santa was soon safely inside the carrier and Tom headed eagerly for the door, obviously impatient to show Santa his new home.

"Thanks very much," Mr Charlton said, shaking hands with Bob.

"Happy Christmas!" Tom called as he followed his dad out into the snow, holding the carrier carefully.

When Tom and Santa had gone, Emily and Alex fed the remaining puppies.

Neil fetched a ball and threw it across the

pen. The three puppies dashed after it, barking eagerly. Then they raced round and round their pen, chasing the ball, each other and their own tails until at last they flopped down, worn out from so much exercise. Once again, Holly chose to settle down beside Alex, with her head and front paws on Alex's foot.

"She's really fond of you," Neil pointed out.

Alex looked down sadly at the tiny puppy. "She's lovely," she said, "but I just don't want another dog. It's no use trying to persuade me."

"I felt like that when my dog Sam died," Neil began. He thought back to that terrible day when Sam's weak heart had finally failed after he'd rescued Jake from drowning. "But—"

"Look, Emily told me about that," Alex interrupted. "And I'm sorry about Sam. But it's not the same. You already had Jake. I didn't have another dog . . ." She broke off, obviously trying to make sense of her feelings. "It wouldn't be fair to Daisy," she said at last. Her eyes filled with tears and she brushed them away. "She was the best dog ever."

Emily put her arm round her. "Daisy wouldn't—"

She didn't get a chance to finish because the door of the rescue centre opened and Jake

Fielding came in. He was a tall young man who wore his long hair in a ponytail. He had a camera slung round his neck and a tripod under his arm. "Your dad said I'd find you in here," he said. "I've come to take some pictures of these pups of yours for the paper."

"Hi, Jake," said Neil. "Thanks for coming." He grinned at him, but inside he was feeling even more frustrated. What a shame Jake had arrived at that moment! Neil was pretty sure that he and Emily could have convinced Alex to take Holly if they hadn't been interrupted.

"Can you each hold one of the puppies, please?" Jake said as Neil let him into the pen. He quickly set up his tripod and attached his camera to the top.

Emily picked up Holly and plonked her in Alex's arms. Then she scooped up Candy, leaving Neil to hold Cracker.

"Cor, we must be overfeeding you," joked Neil as he picked him up. "You weigh a ton." The puppy nudged Neil with his nose, then stared at the camera.

"Move in closer together," Jake said, bending over to look through the camera's viewfinder. There was a flash as he took the picture.

Holly whimpered. "It's all right, girl," Alex

said soothingly.

"I'll just take a couple more," said Jake. His camera flashed again. "Our readers will be pleased to see how well they're looking." He took a final photo then put his camera back in its case and folded up his tripod. "Thanks very much, you lot. They'll be in this week's paper."

"Let's hope it does the trick," Neil said as he placed Cracker in the basket.

He watched Alex put Holly down beside her brother. She stroked Holly's head gently. The chocolate-brown Labrador rolled over and Alex tickled her tummy.

Neil looked at Emily and they both shook their heads. When was Alex going to realize that she and Holly were made for each other?

Chapter Six

"Jet's so well trained," said Neil admiringly as Bob parked the Range Rover outside the church later that afternoon. He watched the vicar's black Labrador nose around the snowy headstones. "He never goes out of the churchyard, you know, even when the gate's open."

"Does he live here, then?" Alex asked in surprise.

"He's the vicar's dog," Neil explained. "He's got his own dog flap so he can come and go as he pleases." He pointed to the back door of the vicarage, which was just visible through the trees on the far side of the churchyard.

Bob opened the car door. "Come on, you lot!

No slacking! There's work to be done."

Jake tried to scramble over into the front seat but Neil held him back. "Not that way, Jake," he laughed. "Wait your turn!" He climbed out and Jake dashed after him. Emily and Alex followed with the bag of presents.

As they went into the churchyard, Jet came bounding over. Jake sniffed Jet, then sprang away from him and disappeared behind an old weather-beaten gravestone, barking playfully. Jet stared after him for a moment, as though he was trying to decide whether to play or not. He soon made up his mind, and bounded after the younger dog.

Neil, Emily and Alex watched the two dogs darting in and out of a row of yew trees in a boisterous game of tag. "Jake seems to have cheered Jet up!" Emily laughed. She picked up the bag of presents. "Let's get started on this grotto."

"I'll have to leave you to it, I'm afraid," said Bob. "I've got to get some shopping but I'll be back later."

"Last minute Christmas presents, by any chance?" Neil said curiously.

Bob grinned. "Never you mind. You just go and get cracking on that grotto." He went out of the churchyard, shutting the gate behind him.

Neil led the way through the heavy door of the church porch, which Gavin always kept unlocked in the daytime. From there they went through a side door into the stone church hall, which was hundreds of years old, but felt light and airy inside.

Emily put the sack of presents down by the door, making sure that it was left ajar so that Jake could get in and out. They found a stepladder and an artificial Christmas tree leaning against a wall. In the middle of the polished wooden floor was a carved chair, a fold-up screen and a stack of cardboard boxes filled with Christmas decorations.

"It looks like Gavin's got all the gear together," said Neil. "If we set the screen up over here, Dad can sit behind it." He carried it to the end of the room and opened it out. "People can go in at one end, have a chat with Dad and collect their present, then come out at the other end."

"I'm going to start decorating the Christmas tree," Emily said. "It'll look nice in front of that screen."

"I'll give you a hand," Alex offered eagerly. She rummaged through one of the boxes and pulled out lengths of gold and silver foil. "Hey! These will look great fixed to the screen, Neil. We just need some drawing pins. . ."

By the time Jake came trotting in from the churchyard, the screen and ceiling were draped with glittering foil and the Christmas tree was transformed into a magical creation of glowing lights, gleaming baubles and shimmering tinsel. Neil thought it looked fantastic.

The Border collie stopped in the doorway and stared curiously. The Christmas tree lights were reflected in his dark eyes. "What do you think then, Jake?" Emily asked, stroking him.

Jake barked once, as though he approved of what he saw, then he pushed past Emily and thrust his head inquisitively into one of the cardboard boxes. When he emerged, strands of silver foil hung from his ears.

Neil laughed. "He didn't want to be outdone by a Christmas tree, did you, Jake?" he said from the stepladder where he was fixing a star to the top of the tree.

"I think he looks sweet," chuckled Alex.

Jake turned his attention to another box. It had higher sides than the first box and he couldn't see into it. Suddenly he jumped up and rested his front paws on the edge of the box.

"Don't do that!" Neil cried. His warning came too late – the box toppled over, spilling its contents over the startled dog.

Jake jumped back. A string of fairy lights was draped across his back now, and scattered around him there were baubles, silver bells and plastic reindeers and snowmen.

"Here, Jake," Neil called, climbing down from the ladder. Jake trotted across to him, trailing the lights. Laughing, Neil lifted the light cable off the young dog's back and brushed the foil strands from his ears.

"I wonder where Jet's got to," said Emily.

"I hope he's gone back into the vicarage," Neil said. "If Jake can cause this much mayhem on his own, imagine what two dogs could get up to!"

Alex stood the box upright and began to pile the decorations into it. "We could hang these snowmen and reindeer from the coat hooks," she suggested. "And the lights could go round the door."

"Good idea," Emily said, picking up two of the snowmen and hanging them on hooks. She stood back to admire the effect.

"There's a socket behind the door," Neil said, "so we'll be able to plug in the lights."

Suddenly they heard footsteps in the church porch and Jake darted out of the hall. "How are you getting on?" Bob called.

"Come and see, Dad," said Emily.

"Fantastic," Bob said enthusiastically as he looked around. "Have you put the presents behind that screen?"

"No, they're still in the porch," said Emily. "I left them by the door because I thought they'd get in the way while we were decorating."

"But you've brought some of them in here?" Bob persisted.

Neil shook his head. "No. We'll bring them in now. We're going to arrange them around your chair."

Bob looked concerned.

"What's wrong?" Neil asked anxiously.

"Come and see," said Bob grimly, ushering them out of the hall.

The sack containing the presents was still beside the door where Emily had left it. But as he drew near, Neil could see that it was half empty. "Hey, what's happened? Where have all the presents gone?"

"I suppose someone must have taken them," Bob said, puzzled.

"You mean, stolen them!" said Neil angrily.

"The thief must have come into the porch while we were working on the grotto," Emily said miserably. "We wouldn't have heard the door because I left it open for Jake – and we were all talking anyway."

"But who'd steal Christmas presents from a church?" asked Alex. "That's a horrible thing to do."

"The presents might not have been stolen," Bob said in a calm voice. "You mustn't jump to conclusions."

Neil looked round. "You don't think the thief is still here, do you?"

"He would have run off when he heard Dad

coming," Emily said. "But maybe we can find his footprints in the snow and see which way he's gone."

"It's worth a try," said Neil. He whistled for Jake and went outside, with Emily and Alex close behind him.

But the path through the churchyard had been well trampled. There were several sets of footprints on it and trying to distinguish one set from another was an impossible task.

"What I don't understand is why the thief only took some of the presents?" Alex said thoughtfully. "If he heard your dad coming, surely he could have picked up the whole sack and run off with it."

Neil nodded. Alex was right. "Maybe he's planning to come back for the rest of the presents when we've gone home," he said. "He could be hiding somewhere nearby, keeping an eye on us."

Neil scanned the churchyard and started to make his way towards the road to see if he could spot anyone suspicious-looking there. Suddenly he heard a cough behind him. He whirled round, heart thudding. Gavin was walking towards him. "Sorry, Neil," he said. "I didn't mean to startle you. How are you getting on with the grotto?"

Neil told the vicar about the missing presents. Gavin shook his head, perplexed. "It must be a misunderstanding. I'm sure nobody would steal little presents like that."

When Neil had checked the road, they headed back to the church hall, lost in thought.

"Has Neil told you about the missing presents?" Emily asked.

Gavin nodded. "But I'm sure there's a perfectly innocent explanation. Let's have a look at Santa's grotto," he said cheerfully.

Neil led the way back to the hall.

"Oh, you've done a wonderful job," the vicar said, clearly impressed.

"It's all been a waste of time, though," Neil said glumly. "The grotto will have to be cancelled if there aren't enough presents for Father Christmas to give out."

"I'll get some more," Gavin said. "People have been looking forward to this, and I can't cancel it now."

"But you won't make any money for the roof repairs if you have to buy more presents," said Emily.

"I'll be happy to supply dog treats, Gavin," Bob offered.

"Thanks, Bob. That's kind of you. That means I only need to buy presents for the children." Gavin smiled at Emily. "Don't look so worried. We'll still make a little bit of profit, it just won't be as much as I'd hoped."

"I think we should hide the rest of the presents," said Neil, "just in case the thief comes back."

"We could tuck some into the Christmas tree," Alex suggested. "If we push them in far enough, they'll be hidden in the branches."

"Good idea. And if we leave the hall door open, we can put some parcels behind it." Neil scooped up an armful of presents and positioned them behind the door. Then he pushed the door back against the wall to hide the parcels, while Emily stuffed the remainder under the cushion on Father Christmas's chair.

"I've got some good news," Gavin said, when they'd finished.

"Oh, we forgot!" said Emily. "Has Susie had the baby?"

Gavin beamed round at them. "A boy. Joshua."

"Congratulations, Gavin," Bob cried, slapping him on the back.

"Thanks." Gavin looked at his watch. "I must

get a move on. I only popped home to feed Jet and take him for a walk. I want to get back to the hospital as soon as I can."

"We could feed Jet for you, if you like," suggested Neil. "And then we could take him for a long run."

Gavin's smile broadened. "That would be wonderful, Neil. Thanks." He handed Neil his back door key. "I've got a key to the front door, so post this one through the letterbox after you've locked up." He hurried away.

"I ought to go too," Alex said. "My parents will be wondering where I've got to."

"Right, I'll give you a lift, Alex," said Bob. "You two can walk back after you've seen to Jet."

"OK," Neil agreed. He whistled for Jake, and he and Emily wound their way round the gravestones to Gavin's back door.

"I wonder who did steal the presents," Emily said. "They can't be worth very much."

"Whoever it is will get a shock when he unwraps them," Neil said, with a chuckle. "Imagine his face when he finds out he's stolen a load of rubber bones and dog biscuits!"

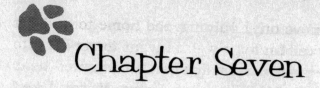

Chapter Seven

Alex was on the doorstep of King Street Kennels just after nine o'clock the next morning. "I hope you don't mind . . . I wanted to see the puppies."

Neil was overjoyed. Perhaps, at last, she was ready to admit that she wanted Holly. Not that she looked particularly happy, he thought as he led the way through the house to the back door.

"I want to say goodbye to them," explained Alex sadly. "I expect they'll all be gone soon and my mum said I'd be upset if I hadn't seen Holly for one last time . . . She's probably right."

Neil felt a rush of sympathy for Alex as he pulled on his coat and boots. "Come on then," he said gently, leading the way across the snowy yard.

The puppies were lying in a contented heap in their basket, fast asleep, when Neil and Alex went into the rescue centre. "They're so sweet," Alex said wistfully, watching them through the wire netting.

At the sound of Alex's voice, Holly opened her eyes. She jumped out of the basket and raced across to the wire. "She's pleased to see you," said Neil. He paused, then added, "She does seem to respond to you more than to anyone else, you know." Just seeing the two of them

together made Neil feel hopeful again. If anyone could persuade Alex to take Holly, it was the pup herself.

Holly pressed against the wire, whining a greeting. Alex pushed her fingers through and stroked Holly's silky chest. The Labrador pup licked her hand, then tried to scramble up the inside of the wire towards Alex's face, her tail wagging vigorously.

Neil let Alex into the pen, then started to prepare the puppies' food. Alex sat on the floor with Holly curled up in her lap. She was stroking the pup's chocolate-brown fur while Holly gazed up at her.

Neil took the food into the pen and Cracker and Candy woke up. They leapt joyfully out of their basket and raced across to the bowl, yapping with excitement. Holly stood up on Alex's lap. She hesitated for a moment, watching Alex intently. "Go and get your breakfast, girl," Alex said, giving her a gentle push.

Holly jumped down and ran to the bowl, nudging her way in between her brother and sister.

"They're great, aren't they?" said Neil.

Alex smiled. "Especially Holly. She seems so

friendly and intelligent. I bet she'd be really easy to train and—" She broke off and a look of dismay flashed across her face.

Neil groaned inwardly. One moment he was sure Alex would take Holly, the next he was sure she wouldn't. "Having another dog wouldn't make you forget Daisy," he said at last.

Alex stood up. "No," she said firmly. "I don't want another dog. It would be . . . disloyal." She headed for the door of the pen but before she reached it, the outer door of the rescue centre opened and Bob showed a middle-aged couple in. "Ah, Neil. There you are," he said. "Mr and Mrs Grant have come to choose a puppy. They'd like a female one."

Alex froze. Then she turned and looked back at Holly, her face stiff with anxiety.

"Aren't they adorable?" said Mrs Grant.

Neil let them into the pen and Mrs Grant bent down and called to the puppies. They looked up from their bowl, hesitated, then continued to eat. "They'll probably come to you as soon as they've finished eating," Neil told the Grants. "The golden one and the brown one are both girls."

He turned to Alex. "Look, why don't you take

Holly?" he whispered urgently. "If you don't, someone else will pick her."

"I don't want her." Alex spoke fiercely but her eyes were sad.

"The brown one's gorgeous," said Mr Grant as Holly trotted away from the bowl. He picked her up. "She looks sturdy and intelligent."

Mrs Grant picked up Candy. "This one's lovely, too," she said, laughing as the pup licked her ear. She turned to her husband. "I can't decide. You pick."

"We'll have this chocolate one then," Mr Grant said.

Alex went pale.

"Actually," said Neil quickly, "that one's already promised to someone. Sorry, I should have made that clear," he mumbled awkwardly. "But the golden puppy – Candy – is just as sweet, don't you think?"

The Grants looked puzzled. "All right," Mr Grant said, putting Holly down gently and giving her a pat. "We'll take Candy instead. The colour's not important and they both seem friendly."

"Our daughter's gone away to college," Mrs Grant explained as Neil showed them out of the rescue centre. Candy was snuggled in her arms

323

and Neil was pleased to see how well she'd taken to her new owner. "We've been lonely without her and we thought a dog would help to fill the gap."

"We're going to bring her to your dad's obedience classes," added Mr Grant as they set off across the yard to the office to sign the forms.

"I'll see you there, then," Neil called after them. He went back into the rescue centre. Alex was holding Holly in her arms. As Neil drew near, he saw that she was close to crying.

"Who's Holly promised to?" Alex asked in a wobbly voice.

"You, if you want her," said Neil gently. "But we really can't keep her for ever, Alex. The next time somebody wants her, we'll have to let her go." He picked up Cracker and made a fuss of him.

Alex nodded and blinked her tears away. "I know and I don't want her," she said decisively. "I really don't." She put Holly down in the basket and went out of the pen. "And anyway, my grandad phoned last night. He thinks he knows someone who might like one of them."

"That's great," said Neil. He put Cracker down beside his water bowl and followed Alex out, shaking his head in confusion.

"I don't believe it – the thief has been here again!" Emily cried. "I left four presents under this cushion and now there are only two." Neil, Emily and Alex had decided to go back to the grotto to check on the presents and to see if they could find any clues to the identity of the thief.

Alex ran to the Christmas tree. "One's been taken from here as well," she said, dismayed.

"But how on earth did the thief know where to look?" Neil asked, mystified. He looked behind the door, and sure enough, one of the presents he'd left there had vanished as well.

They exchanged puzzled looks. "Why did he only take some of the presents again?" Emily asked.

"And this is weird, too," Neil said. "It hasn't snowed since last night but I noticed that there was only one set of footprints leading to and from the church. They must be Gavin's so where are the thief's?"

Emily and Alex followed him to the church door. Neil pointed to the tracks. "See?" he said. "Those footprints lead from the vicarage to the church and back again. And there are Jet's pawprints beside them – although he was obviously running around a bit because his tracks go all over the place."

"So the thief must have come back before last night's snowfall," Alex said.

Neil nodded. "It looks like it. Let's go and ask Gavin if he noticed anything yesterday when he locked up the church for the night."

They hurried to the vicarage and rang the bell. "Hello, you lot," said Gavin as he opened the door for them. "I was just about to go to the hospital to pick up Susie and Joshua. What can I do for you?"

"Some more presents have disappeared from the grotto," Neil said.

Gavin frowned. "You're joking!" he said. "Even after you'd hidden them? I know they were all there last night when I locked up because I checked them."

Neil looked thoughtful. "So that means they must have been taken during the night."

"But the church was locked in the night," said Gavin. "I don't understand how anyone could have got in . . . Look, I've really got to go now. I'll have to leave you to solve the mystery."

Neil, Emily, Alex and Jake made their way back to the church and examined the door for signs of a break-in. But both the door and the lock were undamaged, the windows couldn't be opened, and none of the panes of glass had been smashed.

"He must have a key then," Neil said. "It's the only explanation."

"I know! Why don't we put a sackful of paper by the door, to see if we can lure him into coming back today," suggested Alex.

"Good idea," said Neil, leading the way back to the grotto. He rummaged in the boxes of decorations. "This will do," he said, pulling out some sheets of dog-eared Christmas wrapping paper.

They filled the bag with balls of paper and Neil placed it in the doorway. "Let's hide and keep watch for a bit. The thief must have come at about this time yesterday so it's worth a try," he said. He patted Jake. "How about it, boy? Do you fancy a bit of doggy detective work."

Jake gave an eager bark and jumped up, putting his front paws on Neil's chest.

"Good for you," laughed Neil.

"Where shall we hide?" asked Emily.

They looked round. "Somewhere near the door," Neil said, "so that we can see people coming and going." He pointed to a huge, ancient gravestone that was covered in moss. "That one looks big enough to hide us all."

As they crouched down behind it, Jet trotted up. "Hello, boy," Emily said. "Have you come to help?"

Jet wagged his tail and squeezed in between Emily and Alex while Jake pressed against Neil. "At least we've got the dogs to keep us warm," Neil said in a low voice. "It's freezing out here." Though he was wearing gloves, his fingers were already numb with cold and he rubbed his hands together vigorously.

"As long as they don't make a noise and give us away," said Alex.

They settled down to watch. Out on the road a lorry drove past, puffing out a cloud of dirty exhaust fumes. Birds huddled together on the church roof and they saw an occasional shopper pass by, laden down with bulging bags. But nobody came into the churchyard.

Jake and Jet grew impatient with the long wait and wandered off to play. Neil could see them now and then, darting in and out amongst the headstones.

Time passed slowly. Grey clouds were beginning to build up overhead. "I think it's going to snow again," Alex said at last.

They all stared at the sky. "Let's give up and go home," said Emily, her teeth chattering. "I'm frozen." She came out from behind the gravestone and Alex followed her, looking relieved.

Neil stood up and stretched his cramped legs. "Yeah, I guess you're right. It doesn't look as though he's coming back today," he admitted reluctantly. He was frustrated that they hadn't been able to solve the mystery. Keeping watch at night seemed a better bet, though. Surely the thief was more likely to come back then – when he would be pretty sure that there would be no one around to see what he was up to. . .

"I'm coming back tonight," said Neil decisively.

"What, by yourself?" asked Alex.

Neil nodded.

"I'll come with you," Emily offered.

"There's no point in both of us getting frozen. And there's no point in Mum and Dad getting cross with both of us if they find out, either."

"But it'll be dark. And you'll be in a graveyard," Alex persisted.

"So?" Neil shrugged. "I've got to get to the bottom of this."

"Won't you be scared?" asked Alex.

"I'll have Jake with me," Neil pointed out. He whistled and the Border collie came running up to him obediently.

"Come on," Emily said impatiently. "If we don't go home soon, I'm going to turn into an icicle."

Snow began to fall, driven across the churchyard by an icy wind. "You won't come back tonight if it's snowing like this, will you?" Alex asked, shivering.

"Of course I will," said Neil. He wouldn't let a bit of bad weather put him off. He was determined to catch the thief, and nothing was going to stop him.

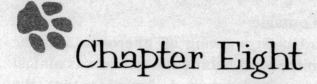

Chapter Eight

Neil's alarm clock rang at midnight. He leapt up, startled by the loudness of it, then reached out and switched it off. The house felt cold as he climbed out of bed, and he got ready quickly, shivering uncontrollably.

When he was dressed Neil picked up his torch, opened his bedroom door a crack and listened. The house was silent. Neil tiptoed along the landing and down the stairs.

Jake was asleep in the kitchen. He looked up in surprise when Neil crept in but he stood up and trotted to greet him all the same. "Good boy, Jake," Neil said, clipping on his lead. He unlocked the back door and he and Jake

331

slipped outside.

It had been snowing all afternoon and the snow in the yard behind the house was almost knee-deep. Neil frowned, knowing that the tracks he and Jake left would give him away unless it snowed again after he got home. Still, he was determined to go ahead with his plan. He set off with his woollen hat pulled down over his ears and his collar turned up, but the icy wind still cut right through him.

Once he reached the churchyard, he hesitated. By day it had been easy to say that he wouldn't be scared, but now the moon cast an eerie glow across the snow-covered headstones and he began to feel uneasy. He looked round anxiously. Everything was still. Tentatively, he pushed the gate open and went inside.

Neil held Jake's collar as he made his way between the graves, glad of the Border collie's company. He reached the huge gravestone near the church door, brushed away the snow from behind it and sat down to wait. The gravestone offered some protection from the wind and, with Jake pressed up against him, Neil began to warm up a little.

"Let's hope he comes soon, Jake," he whispered. Jake whined and twisted his head so that he could lick Neil's cheek.

The long, silent night wore on but nobody came. At one point Neil heard two men talking softly as they walked along the road towards the church. He stiffened and waited expectantly, but they passed by.

Neil began to feel sleepy. He shifted his position, knowing it would be dangerous to fall asleep in the cold, but it was hard to stay awake with nothing to do but stare into the darkness. And it seemed to be getting darker. Neil glanced up at the sky. Most of the stars had been blotted out by clouds and the moon was half covered too. He groaned inwardly. Surely it wasn't going to snow again. Still, at least his tracks would be covered up if it did . . . .

Sure enough, snow began to fall. Neil switched on his torch, hunching over it to shield the light from anyone who might be watching, and looked at his watch. It was ten past two. He switched the torch off again and willed the thief to come. "We'll give him another quarter of an hour, Jake," he whispered. "Then we'll go home."

Jake leapt up.

"What is it, boy?" Neil reached for Jake's collar, but before he could get hold of it, the young dog dashed away around the side of the church.

"Jake!" Neil hissed. "Come back!" He scrambled up, knowing he'd got to find Jake. If he *had* heard, the thief the Border collie could be in danger. Quickly switching on his torch, Neil charged after him.

The churchyard was shadowy. Neil whirled his torch round, desperately looking for Jake, but the snow was falling fast now and the flakes got into his eyes. He brushed them away impatiently as he ran between the gravestones, swinging the torch from left to right. "Jake,

where are you?" he called softly.

Suddenly Neil saw a dark shape dart behind a gravestone on the far side of the churchyard. He dashed towards it. "Jake," he hissed. "Here, boy."

Then two shapes shot out of the shadows. Neil jumped with fright, his heart hammering. But he soon relaxed as he swung the torch beam round and saw that it was Jake and Jet. Jake was all right! He must have heard Jet coming out through his dog door and run off to play!

The dogs bounded up to Neil, barking a greeting. "You gave me a scare," he scolded, patting each of them in turn. Then he clipped on Jake's lead. "Come on, you two. There's no point in hanging around here any longer. If the thief was lurking nearby, he'll have run a mile after that performance."

He led Jake to Gavin's back door and Jet trotted along behind. Neil held the dog flap open. "In you go, Jet. It's too cold for you to be out here in the middle of the night."

The black Labrador touched noses with Jake, then pushed through the dog flap. Neil let it close behind him and set off home with Jake.

*

Neil slept late the next morning. When he got downstairs Carole was clearing the breakfast table. "Morning, sleepyhead," she said.

"Morning," said Neil. She didn't look angry, he thought with relief, so she obviously didn't know about his midnight outing yet. He pushed a slice of bread into the toaster.

"Would you like some hot chocolate?" Carole asked.

"Yes, please," Neil said, yawning.

"Guess what?" Emily called, running into the kitchen. "Someone's coming from Manchester to see the puppies. A boy called Michael Todd and his mum. They know Alex's grandad."

"Oh . . . that's good, I suppose," Neil said hesitantly. He knew he should be pleased at the thought of finding a home for another of the puppies but he was worried too. What if they chose Holly? If they did, he knew Alex would be devastated. And if they chose Cracker, and Alex still refused to have Holly, then the puppy would be alone in the rescue centre for Christmas.

"Aren't you pleased?" Emily asked.

"I am really," Neil began. "It's just—"

"I know," interrupted Emily. "You think it would be best if Holly went to Alex. But it doesn't look like she'll change her mind, and time's running out."

Before Neil could reply, Sarah came rushing into the kitchen, wearing a tinsel ring on her head. "Dad's going to buy the Christmas tree later. And we're going to decorate it after tea. And I'm an angel."

Neil laughed as he spread butter on his toast. "Does that mean you're going to be good?"

"I'm always good," said Sarah indignantly. "Aren't I, Mum?"

"Most of the time," Carole said, setting Neil's mug of hot chocolate down on the worktop. "Here you are, Neil. I'll be out in Kennel Block One. Can you give me a shout when the people from Manchester get here?" She pulled on her coat and went out.

Neil looked outside, hoping she wouldn't notice the tracks he and Jake had left the night before, but the snow in the yard was deeper than ever and he knew that they would have been filled in.

Just then the front doorbell rang and Neil ran to answer it.

Alex was on the step. "Hi," she said. "I've come to see how you got on last night."

Neil shook his head. "No luck. Jake and I

waited for ages but no one showed up." As he stood aside to let her come in, a car pulled into the drive.

Alex looked round.

"We're expecting some people from Manchester," Neil explained. "They know your grandad and they want one of the puppies." He saw Alex's face cloud over. "Look – I can tell them that Holly's already promised to you, if you want. You've still got time to change your mind—"

"No, thanks," Alex interrupted, looking down at the ground.

"Come on!" said Emily, racing past them. "Oh, hello, Alex. Let's go and show the puppies to the Todds."

A woman and a boy of about eight climbed out of the car parked in the courtyard. Neil stopped to talk to them while Alex and Emily went on ahead to the rescue centre.

Just then Carole came out of Kennel Block One. "I thought I heard a car," she said, smiling. "You must be Mrs Todd. Thanks for coming. Did you have a difficult journey?"

Mrs Todd laughed wryly. "It could have been better," she said, "but we're here now. That's the main thing. Michael's been over the moon since he found out we were getting another dog."

Michael, a serious-looking boy with glasses and dark cropped hair, tugged his mother's hand. "Can we see the puppies now, Mum? Please."

"Of course you can," Carole said as she led the way to the rescue centre.

Emily and Alex were already inside. Alex was throwing a ball for Holly and the puppy was scampering after it. Cracker was lying in the basket, watching his sister's antics lazily.

Neil unfastened the pen and he and Michael went inside. Alex watched Michael anxiously as he looked from Holly to Cracker and back again. "They're lovely, aren't they?" he said. Holly charged towards him with the ball in her mouth and he stooped down to stroke her. Cracker got to his feet slowly, and padded over to meet the newcomer too.

"Shep, my last puppy, was run over," Michael said sadly, glancing at Alex and Emily. "It was terrible. I thought I'd never want another dog but I've changed my mind now. I still miss Shep but it's horrible not having a dog at home." He grinned at the girls. "Which one do you want?"

Emily glanced at Alex. Neil knew that she

was hoping Alex would tell him she'd chosen Holly – but Alex didn't say anything.

"We're not here to choose a puppy," Emily said at last. "I live here – and Alex is my friend."

Carole and Mrs Todd came towards the pen, chatting. "Of course Michael was devastated when Shep was run over," Mrs Todd was saying. "But there are so many dogs in need of good homes that it seems a shame not to have another one. Michael soon got used to the idea."

"I agree," Carole said. "Committed dog owners are hard to find."

Neil watched Alex's face. She looked guilty and confused. Perhaps seeing Michael choose a new puppy after the death of his old dog would finally help her to feel OK about adopting Holly.

"Have you chosen, Michael?" Mrs Todd asked.

Michael reached out a hand to both puppies. Cracker rolled over to have his tummy stroked. Holly darted to Alex, dropped the ball and tugged at her shoelace. "I think this black one has chosen me," Michael said, grinning. He picked up the puppy and held him against his chest. "He's great, isn't he, Mum?"

"He certainly is," agreed Mrs Todd.

Neil waited until the Todds and Carole had

gone out of the rescue centre to fill in the paperwork, then he turned to Alex. "I think Holly has chosen you, Alex."

Alex blushed. "I shouldn't have come," she said sadly. "It's not fair to Holly. She might want to live with me but I can't have her." She opened the door of the pen and started to walk away. "I won't come again. And I hope you hurry up and find somebody to take her," she called.

Emily raced after her. Neil picked Holly up. He didn't want the little puppy to be alone just yet. It would probably take her a while to adjust to life without any brothers or sisters. "That's it, then, girl," he said sadly. "I've done my best but Alex just isn't going to see that the two of you belong together."

Holly's eyes began to close. Gently Neil laid her in her basket. "We'll just have to find someone else to love you," he said with a sigh.

Chapter Nine

"Enjoy yourself, Father Christmas," Carole called from the doorstep as Bob unlocked the Range Rover. "I hope the grotto's a success." Neil, Emily, Sarah and Jake piled into the back and Alex got into the front seat.

"Enjoy myself? There's not much chance of that!" Bob replied with a grin. "I mean, think of that beard!"

"You'll be fine," Carole assured him.

"Are you sure you don't want to come, Mum?" asked Emily.

Carole shook her head. "There's too much to do here. Bev and Kate have been working flat out to prepare for our Christmas boarders, and one of us ought to be around to give them a hand."

Bob started the engine and manoeuvred the Range Rover carefully through the snow to the end of the drive. "The roads don't look too bad," he said as he turned towards Compton. "I thought we'd have to walk to the church when I got up this morning – it must have been snowing most of the night."

"It's a shame the real Father Christmas couldn't come," sighed Sarah.

"He's too busy getting ready for tomorrow night," Neil explained. "He's probably starting to load the sleigh already."

Sarah giggled with excitement. "I wish Christmas would hurry up. I can't wait to see what Father Christmas brings me." She suddenly became serious. "I won't tell anybody you're not the real Father Christmas, Dad," she promised.

"Good for you. We don't want people to be disappointed," said Bob as he pulled up outside the church. "Come on, you lot. Let's get a move on. I've still got to get changed."

They hurried to the vicarage and rang the bell. Gavin came to the door. "Hello, Bob, thanks for coming so early," he said gratefully.

He showed Bob into his study, where the Father Christmas suit was hanging, and left him to get changed. "Why don't the rest of you come into the warm kitchen?"

Jet was lying by the stove. He lifted his head and looked at them as they came in, then flopped down again. "He doesn't look too lively," Neil said, crouching down to pat him.

Gavin frowned. "He's been a bit low lately."

Sarah went to stroke the black Labrador. "He's really excited about seeing Father Christmas," she said. Then she added in a whisper, "He doesn't know it's only Dad dressed up." Jake trotted over to her, and lay down beside Jet with his head resting on the older dog's back.

"Oh, I nearly forgot," said Neil suddenly. "We've brought a few posters with us advertising the last of our Labrador puppies. Would you mind if we put them up in the grotto?"

"Not at all," Gavin said.

Susie, Gavin's wife, came into the kitchen. "I thought I heard voices," she said, beaming round at them.

"Hello," said Emily. "How's Joshua?"

"He's fine – he's asleep upstairs. Would you

all like to see him?"

"Oh yes, please!" Emily said enthusiastically.

Neil couldn't see why anyone would get so excited about seeing a new baby. If Gavin and Susie had a new puppy, that would be different . . .

As they went out of the kitchen, Jake got up to follow them. "You stay here, Jake," Neil commanded.

"It's all right," said Susie. "Jake can come too, if he likes. Joshua's got to get used to dogs."

"Come on then, Jake," Neil said. "But be quiet. You'll be in trouble if you wake the baby."

Susie led the way upstairs. "He's in here," she said softly. A double bed occupied most of the floor space but there was a wicker crib standing beside it. "Go in and have a look at him," said Susie. "I'm just going to run myself a bath."

They crept into the room and gathered round the crib. The baby was fast asleep, his downy blond hair standing up in wisps and his tiny hands clutching his quilt. "Isn't he lovely?" Alex whispered.

"I wish we could take him home," said Sarah.

Suddenly, Neil heard a rustling and

crunching sound behind him. Leaving the girls to admire Joshua, he turned quickly, worried that Jake was up to mischief. The Border collie was lying half under Gavin and Susie's bed. He seemed to be chewing something.

"What have you got there, Jake?" Neil hissed. He bent down to see, then drew back in astonishment. Jake was chewing a rubber bone wrapped in paper. Neil recognized it. It was one of the presents from the church.

"Where did you get that? Come out of there." As Jake slunk out from under the bed, Neil saw that there were more presents there. Hardly able to believe his eyes, he bent down to have a proper look. There was no doubt about it. The missing presents were piled under the vicar's bed!

Neil took the rubber bone away from Jake, then sat back on his heels to think. Surely Gavin hadn't stolen the presents himself. But what other explanation could there be? The last place a thief would think to hide them would be in the vicarage.

He looked round to see if anyone else had noticed but Emily, Sarah and Alex were still peering at the baby.

Just then Jet came into the bedroom. To Neil's surprise, he was carrying one of the presents from the grotto in his mouth. He squirmed under the bed, deposited the present on the pile and wriggled out again. Then he lay down beside Neil, looking rather pleased with himself.

"Jet's the thief!" Neil cried.

"What?" said Emily, whirling round in astonishment. "He can't be!"

"He is." Neil showed her the heap of presents. "He just brought one in and added it to the pile."

"The baby's waking up," Alex said.

Neil's hand flew to his mouth. "I'd forgotten all about him."

Joshua began to cry and Susie rushed into the bedroom and picked him up.

"Sorry," Neil apologized. "It was my fault. I'd just discovered what had happened to your missing presents and I forgot that I had to be quiet."

"What do you mean?" asked Gavin, coming into the room.

Neil pointed to the bed. "They're here – Jake found them. It looks like Jet's been taking them all along."

Gavin bent down and peered under the bed. He ruffled Jet's fur. "What on earth have you been up to, Jet?" He pulled out a few of the presents. "They look all right," he said. "I should be able to take the second lot I bought back to the shop and get a refund."

"The dogs will get more exciting presents, too, rather than just dog treats," Neil said.

"And the grotto will make some money for the church hall roof repairs," said Emily.

Gavin smiled. "Yes, it will. And it's all thanks to you, Neil, and to Jake."

"How did Jet take the presents during the night, though?" asked Alex. "The church is closed then."

Gavin looked thoughtful. "Well, he came with me when I went to lock up. I was there for a while, sorting a few things out, so I suppose he could have taken them then. He must have gone backwards and forwards from the church hall to the house to steal all those presents, though – and without me even noticing."

"We saw that he'd left lots of tracks in the snow," Emily said.

"And being a dog, he'd be able to sniff the presents out," Neil added, "even after we'd hidden them. Does he usually take things?"

Gavin shook his head. "Not that I know of."

"So why has he suddenly started it now?" asked Neil, thinking out loud.

"He's been a bit moody and depressed lately," Gavin said. "And I've been feeling bad because I haven't had time to walk him much."

"He's probably been stealing to get your attention then," Neil said knowledgeably. "He must feel a bit left out. Dogs often feel like that when there's a new baby in the family."

"Oh, poor Jet!" cried Susie. She called him and the Labrador trotted eagerly to her. "We still love you, boy," she said, rubbing the side of

349

his head with her free hand. The big dog's tail wagged happily.

"Let's get the presents out," Gavin said, lying down and reaching under the bed.

Suddenly they heard a voice from downstairs. "Ho ho ho!"

"It's Father Christmas!" cried Sarah.

"It's Dad," Neil laughed. They all carried an armful of presents downstairs. Bob was standing in the hall, dressed in his Father Christmas outfit. His face was almost hidden by a white beard, which was even bushier than his real one. "How do I look?" he asked.

Jake sat at Bob's feet and gazed up at him with his head on one side, as though he couldn't work out why Bob was dressed in such strange clothes. Neil burst out laughing.

"It's not that bad, is it?" Bob asked.

"Worse!" Neil grinned. He put the presents down on the hall table. "I wouldn't want to be seen in an outfit like that."

"It wouldn't fit you anyway," Sarah said, taking Bob's hand protectively and scowling at Neil.

"But the elf suit would," said Bob. He turned to Gavin. "That elf suit you've got hanging in your study looks exactly the right size for Neil."

Neil stared at his dad in horror. "No way!" he said. "I'm not dressing up as an elf for anybody."

"But Gavin got it out specially for you," Bob persisted, with a twinkle in his eye.

Neil shook his head firmly. "Absolutely not!"

Emily, Alex and Sarah laughed. "Make him wear it, Dad," begged Emily. "Then we can take a picture of him and hang it up at home for everyone to see."

Alex glanced at her watch. "The grotto's meant to be opening in a few minutes," she reminded them. "Do you think we ought to get over to the church hall?"

They went out into the snow, with Jake and Jet bounding ahead of them. A queue of people and dogs were waiting outside. They cheered when they saw Father Christmas. Neil recognized most of them. He stopped to speak to Doctor Harvey and to make a fuss of his two dogs, Finn and Sandy. Mr Hamley, Neil's head teacher, was in the queue too, with Dotty his wayward Dalmatian. Neil wished he had time to greet all of the dogs but Gavin was obviously in a hurry to open the grotto.

Bob went into the church hall and sat on the tinsel-covered chair behind the screen. Emily arranged the presents on either side of him – one pile for children and another for dogs – while Alex switched on the fairy lights and Neil hung up the posters with Holly's picture on them. "Let's hope these do the trick," he said to himself.

"Are you ready?" Gavin asked, sticking his head round the door.

"I think so," said Neil. He peered behind the screen. "Good luck, Dad."

"Thanks," Bob said, tugging at his white beard. "This thing is driving me mad already and I haven't even started yet." He chuckled. "I don't know how I let myself get talked into this."

Emily and Alex positioned themselves at the edge of the screen, ready to take the money.

"Ladies, gentlemen, children and dogs," Gavin said from the other side of the door. "I declare this Christmas grotto open." He flung the door wide and people began to flock inside, admiring the Christmas tree and the decorations. A queue quickly formed by the screen and Emily and Alex began to collect the money.

Sarah was working her way around the room, stroking all the dogs and saying hello to schoolfriends. Neil couldn't help smiling as he watched her – she looked ready to burst at having to keep their Father Christmas's true identity a secret.

Looking round the room, he could see excitement on lots of faces. *Only two more days to go!* he thought. Then he spotted the poster of Holly and his happiness evaporated. It wouldn't be much of a Christmas for the Labrador puppy unless they could find her a home.

Chapter Ten

The crowd was finally thinning when Gavin appeared with a tray of tea. "Could you take one of these in to Father Christmas, please, Neil?"

"Right." Neil went behind the screen and waited until Bob's visitor had finished, then he handed him the cup.

"Just what I need!" Bob croaked. "I've said 'Ho ho ho' so many times that I've almost lost my voice."

"How's it going, apart from that?" asked Neil.

Bob fiddled with the white beard. "I'm so hot I feel as though I've been cooked, and this wretched beard is tickling my nose. But I've patted lots of friendly dogs, seen lots of cheerful

354

faces and heard about all the things the children of Compton would like for Christmas. I've nearly run out of presents, though. How many people are still waiting to see me?"

"Only four or five," Neil said. "But one of them is Mrs Jepson. Sugar and Spice are really looking forward to seeing you," he added, laughing.

"Oh no! Spare me!"

"I'll leave you to it," said Neil, with a grin.

A young couple were looking at one of the posters of Holly when he came out from behind the screen. A red setter was sitting listlessly at their feet, her head drooping and her eyes half closed.

Neil went over and crouched down beside her. He held out a hand to her. "Hello, girl. What's up?"

The dog sniffed him half-heartedly, and he patted her gently.

"Your dog doesn't look too happy," Neil said to its owners, standing up.

The couple turned. "I know," the woman said anxiously. "Poor Topsy. We've got a vet's appointment today but a friend of ours thinks she might be lonely." She pointed to the poster. "We've been thinking of getting a puppy to keep her company. That one looks perfect."

Neil hesitated before he replied. He was still secretly hoping that Alex would change her mind. But he knew that they'd run out of time – Holly needed a home now. "I'm the person you need to speak to about the puppy," Neil told the couple eventually. "My name's Neil Parker and I live at King Street Kennels. Holly's a great little dog – really friendly. Do you want to meet her?"

"Yes, we'll go straight away, if that's OK," the man said enthusiastically. "It'll be nice to have a puppy in the house again at Christmas." Neil gave them directions to the kennels and they hurried out of the hall, with Topsy trailing behind them.

As soon as they had gone, Neil raced over to Emily. "That couple are going to have a look at Holl—" He broke off quickly as Alex came out from behind the screen.

She stared at him in shock. "Do you mean they're going to adopt her?" she said in a wobbly voice.

"Yes, I'm afraid so," said Neil, looking at his feet.

Alex's eyes filled with tears. "No! We've got to stop them! Holly's *my* dog. I want her to live with *me*."

"But why didn't you say something before?" asked Neil, exasperated. "We gave you so many chances to change your mind! It's too late now."

"I didn't feel like this before," sobbed Alex. "I mean, I liked Holly but it seemed wrong to want another dog – after Daisy."

Emily smiled sadly at Alex. "There'll be other dogs at the rescue centre. You can always have one of those."

Alex sobbed harder than ever. "I don't want any other dog. I only want Holly." She gripped Neil's arm. "We've got to stop those people. We've got to tell them Holly's already got an owner."

Neil shook his head sadly. "I'm sorry, Alex," he said, "but it's too late. There's nothing we can do now. If they want her, then she's theirs."

Neil stared gloomily out of the window of the Range Rover as Bob drove back to King Street Kennels. Compton was ablaze with coloured lights but Neil hardly noticed them. He was too upset about what had happened.

Beside him, Alex and Emily sat in miserable silence. Even Sarah was subdued.

As Bob reached the kennels, a car turned out of the drive. Neil recognized the young couple inside it – the people he'd spoken to at the grotto. He peered into the car and caught a glimpse of Holly sitting next to the red setter on the back seat.

Alex had seen the puppy too. "It's Holly!" she cried, and burst into tears again.

As Bob parked the car, Carole came out to meet them, smiling. "Holly's gone," she said cheerfully. "Mr and Mrs Biggs have taken her. They seem really nice. Apparently their other dog—" She stopped when she saw Alex's miserable face. "What on earth's wrong?" she asked.

"Alex has realized that she wants Holly, after

all," explained Emily.

"Oh dear, you poor thing," sighed Carole. "Let's go inside and talk about it." She led Alex into the kitchen.

Neil and Emily followed a few moments later, and found Alex sitting at the kitchen table with a box of tissues and a glass of Coke in front of her. They decided that it was best to leave her with their mum, and went through into the sitting room. The Christmas tree stood in the window, glittering brightly.

"It doesn't feel like Christmas any more," Emily said gloomily.

"This whole thing is my fault," said Neil, slumping into a chair beside the fire.

"No, it isn't," Emily said. "You tried to get Alex to take Holly. We both did."

"But I told those people how great Holly is too." Neil seized a cushion and thumped it angrily. "Why didn't I say she'd already got a home? Then Alex could have had her."

Emily sat on the arm of his chair. "Alex insisted she didn't want her," she pointed out. "And we could hardly have kept Holly in the rescue centre for ever, while we waited for Alex to change her mind. Especially not at Christmas."

Sarah came into the room and stood by the Christmas tree, touching the baubles and setting them swinging so that they shone in the firelight. "Why's everybody so grumpy?" she demanded. "It's nearly Christmas."

Neil shrugged. All the excitement he'd been feeling about Christmas had evaporated. Holly and Alex would never be together now and there was nothing Neil could do about it.

Neil woke early on Christmas Eve. He lay staring up at his bedroom ceiling, trying to recapture the Christmas spirit he'd felt at the grotto, but images of Holly and of Alex's tear-streaked face kept crowding into his head.

He decided to get up and take Jake for a run. As usual, the Border collie was eager to go out, so the two of them set off for the ridgeway.

The ground was still thick with snow and the rising sun set it sparkling as though it were scattered with diamonds. It was a fantastic morning, but Neil couldn't really enjoy it – not while his head ached with the misery of knowing Holly and Alex were parted for good.

Neil let Jake off the lead and watched him racing back and forth, throwing up clouds of loose snow at every step.

They climbed steadily. By the time they reached the top of the hill, the sun was up and Compton lay below them, the snowy roofs and gardens looking strangely out of place against the brilliant blue sky behind.

A figure appeared on a path a little way away. Neil recognized her and his heart sank. He'd come here to try to forget about Alex for a while and here she was, walking slowly towards him.

Alex glanced up and saw him. She looked pale and miserable. "Sorry about yesterday," she said.

"How are you feeling?" Neil asked.

She shrugged. "Pretty awful, actually. But I know it was my own stupid fault . . . Look, I really can't stop and talk – Mum and Dad will be wondering where I am." She turned away. "Have a good Christmas."

Neil watched her walk away from him, head down and shoulders drooping. He wished there was something he could do or say that would cheer her up. But he knew it was hopeless.

"Neil!" Emily was dashing up the hill towards him.

"What's wrong?" Neil called.

"Nothing. Well . . . I don't know. Mum and Dad sent me to fetch Alex," Emily panted.

"Why?" asked Neil.

"They wouldn't say," said Emily. "But they looked pretty pleased."

Neil shook his head. "I can't imagine what they could do to cheer her up. I've just seen her and she looks really upset."

"Well, you never know. Go and get her – and hurry up!"

"OK," Neil agreed reluctantly. He caught up with Alex near the path that led into her road. "Wait!" he called.

Alex turned.

"You've got to come to the kennels with me. Mum and Dad need to see you."

"I expect they want me to look at another dog." Alex shook her head. "It's kind of them but I'm not interested." She turned to go.

"Please," Neil said, catching her arm. "They wouldn't have sent Emily to find you if it wasn't important."

Alex shrugged. "OK. But it's a waste of time."

They hurried down to the kennels. Carole and Bob were waiting for them in the kitchen. "What's going on?" Neil asked. He fetched a towel and rubbed Jake's fur dry.

"You'll see." Bob winked at him, then placed a plate of hot, buttered toast on the table. "Tuck into this while you're waiting."

Just then Neil heard a car driving into the yard. Carole ran to the front door and opened it. "They're here!" she cried.

"Who's here?" Neil demanded, standing up.

"Just wait and see," said Bob.

Neil glanced at Emily, hoping that she could explain what was going on, but she looked just as mystified as he felt. They heard Carole inviting somebody to come inside, then a dog's claws clicking along the hall. A moment later, Holly scampered into the kitchen, her tail wagging wildly. She spotted Alex and darted straight to her. Alex stared at the Labrador, her face clouded with uncertainty.

Holly jumped up and Alex bent down to stroke her.

"What's going on?" Neil asked. "Why's Holly here?"

Carole came into the room with Mr and Mrs Biggs, the couple who had adopted Holly. "Mrs Biggs rang earlier," said Carole, "while you were out with Jake."

"That's right," Mr Biggs said. "We took Topsy to the vet last night and it turns out that she's pregnant."

"Pregnant?" Neil repeated. "Of course! That's

363

why she was looking a bit low."

"Yes, I suppose we should have thought of it before, really," said Mr Biggs rather sheepishly.

Suddenly Neil understood what this meant. "So, I suppose you can't really keep Holly now?" he asked tentatively, glancing across at Alex's hopeful face.

"Not really, no. We felt terrible about having to bring Holly back," Mrs Biggs went on. "But we just won't be able to manage her when we've got a litter of pups to see to. And when we rang to explain what had happened, your mum told us that somebody else wanted Holly anyway." She beamed at Alex. "I can see you're already very fond of her. And she obviously loves you."

Alex's eyes shone with joy. She swept the puppy into her arms and hugged her tightly. "Oh Holly, I can hardly believe it," she cried. "Thank you for bringing her back. This is going to be the best Christmas ever!"

The Morgans and Holly came to King Street Kennels for Christmas dinner. As everyone sat down at the table, Neil looked round happily. It had turned out to be a perfect day.

He looked across the kitchen to where Bob was carving the turkey. Jake and Holly were

sitting at his feet, watching hopefully in case he dropped a piece of meat. Mr and Mrs Morgan and Alex seemed happy and relaxed. Through the kitchen window, Neil could see snow falling gently.

"I'm glad you could all come today," Carole said. She filled everyone's glass. "As soon as Bob brings the turkey over, I think we should drink a toast."

They waited expectantly as Bob carried the turkey carefully to the table, stepping over the eager dogs.

Carole raised her glass. "To Alex and Holly.

It's great to see them back together again. And here's to a merry Christmas for all of us."

Neil grinned as they chinked glasses. He looked down at Holly, who was leaning contentedly against Alex's leg, and his smile broadened. For a while it had looked as though this Christmas would be terrible, but in the end it was turning out to be one of the best he'd ever had.

Look out for Puppy Patrol® No. 34:

The Puppy Express

All aboard!

Wherever Sugar and Spice go, trouble is never far behind. They're the most pampered pooches Neil knows – and they've got a very important job to do.

The young Westies are the mascots for a special train – dedicated to the memory of a very brave dog. But someone wants to sabotage their moment of glory. All aboard the puppy express for a very eventful journey!

Look out for Puppy Patrol® No. 36:

Barney's Rescue

Can this pup learn to bark?

Barney's a pup with a problem – he can't bark!
Neil and Emily try everything to teach him to
make a noise, but nothing seems to work.

Then one night a terrible fire breaks out while
everyone is asleep. Will brave Barney be able to
bark an alarm?

Look out for Puppy Patrol® No. 37:

Lost and Found

Where is this puppy hiding?

The Parker family have got new neighbours –
and they hate dogs! Their mum is determined to
close down King Street Kennels. Worse still,
there's a puppy roaming wild on their land. Neil
and Emily don't know what to do.

But when they find the pup they're in for a real
shock. Could he be the key to saving the
Kennels?

Look out for Puppy Patrol® No. 38:

Top Dog!

New York's finest!

Neil and Emily are in New York! The Big Apple is abuzz with news of a lost dog – the famous mascot of the Mets baseball team has disappeared.

Neil and Emily are there to catch up with old friends the Hammonds and their dog Delilah, but the story has them hooked. Can they find the missing mutt?

PUPPY PATROL® titles available from Macmillan Children's Books

The prices shown below are correct at the time of going to press. However, Macmillan Publishers reserve the right to show new retail prices on covers which may differ from those previously advertised.

All Macmillan titles can be ordered at your local bookshop or are available by post from:

**Book Service by Post
PO Box 29, Douglas, Isle of Man IM99 1BQ**

Credit cards accepted. For details:
Telephone: 01624 675137
Fax: 01624 670923
E-mail: bookshop@enterprise.net

Free postage and packing in the UK.
Overseas customers: add £1 per book (paperback)
and £3 per book (hardback).